Mexican Booty

A Lucy Ripken Mystery

J. J. Henderson

JJ Henderson

c d s
BOOKS

New York

Copyright © 2006 by J. J. Henderson

Published by CDS Books

Text design by Ruth Lee-Mui

Library of Congress Cataloging-in-Publication Data

Henderson, J. J.
    Mexican booty : a Lucy Ripken mystery / J.J. Henderson.
        p.   cm.
    ISBN-13: 978-1-59315-288-8 (pbk. : alk. paper)
    ISBN-10: 1-59315-288-4 (pbk. : alk. paper) 1. Women
photographers—Fiction. 2. Indian art—Forgeries—Fiction. 3. Art
thefts—Fiction. 4. Isla Mujeres (Mexico)—Fiction. I. Title.
PS3608.E526M49 2006
813'.6—dc22   2006005801

06 07 08 09 / 10 9 8 7 6 5 4 3 2 1

For DD and Jade

Acknowledgments

Thanks to Adams Taylor and Ruth Slivka-Taylor for tour-guiding me through the aesthetic and commercial worlds of Precolumbian art; to Joe Freitas for best friendship and business savvy; and to Hope Matthiessen et al. at CDS for editing and publishing insight and support.

Mexican Booty

A Lucy Ripken Mystery

1

Photo Fakery

"Skreeeeehonnnkkkk . . . " The roar of a T. Rex, bellowing in frustration as it watched its dinner, a fat Brontosaurus pup, lumber across the primeval swamp to safety beneath its mother's belly, echoed through Lucy Ripken's loft and woke her with a start. Damn, she thought, denied the refuge of her dreams. Another gridlock. Will it ever end?

"Skroooonnnnnnkkkk!" The dinosaur played a variation. Lucy muttered, "Damn," then threw the covers off. She lay naked for a moment, watching the white walls and listening to the roar that rose up from the perpetually jammed intersection of Broome and Broadway below. It was no dinosaur howling but the air horn of an eighteen-wheel behemoth, hauling garbage—New York's chief early twenty-first-century export—from Long Island to Ohio.

With a sigh Lucy swung her feet off her sleeping platform onto the cool, dirty, white linoleum floor. She grabbed her frayed silk robe—the one covered with red roses and silver surfers—slipped it on, and padded over to her desk to fire up the computer. She walked to the other end of the loft, put on coffee water, did her ablutions, strolled the length of the loft snapping up the window shades, and then sat before the machine. The thing hummed softly, ready for action.

What action? That was the problem. She didn't know what to write and she didn't dare a glance at her spam-laden mailbox for fear there would be not one single item, among the daily hundreds, that actually pertained to her. Three of the six magazines that gave her regular work had folded in the last eight months, and the other three had new editors who didn't know her from Lucille Ball. The architects who usually hired her to shoot projects were laying off staff, downsizing, and scrambling to survive the dicey economic weather. It wasn't like she could just sit down and start pounding out a novel, for God's sake. There was rent to pay.

Yikes, rent! What was the date? She had a look at her calendar, pinned on the wall and still stuck in March. She tore it off and tracked down to the last Tuesday in April. The 27th. That meant she'd have to come up with $900 next week. Everybody told her how lucky she was to have a 1,300-square-foot loft in SoHo for such cheap rent, but it still represented a fair chunk of cash to her. Here it was due again. Bloody landlord. Whatever she saved in rent she paid out in legal fees, anyway. The evil-tempered little creep had been trying to evict her for seven years and still the case dragged on, the loft board shuffled its feet, the lawyers filed another round of papers, and she and her fellow tenants—there were seven living units in the four upper floors of the six-story building—dangled in limbo, immovable but not entirely legal dwellers in a building zoned for commerce only.

Where Lucy lived had once been the Cherokee Zipper Company, or so the faded sign on her front door told her. It had inspired her to call her photography business Cherokee Productions. Or, at present, Cherokee Non-Productions, since she hadn't had a paying job in three weeks, and her bank balance had reached the low three figures.

Lucy sat and stared at the computer screen, fingers on the keyboard, brain blank, battling the urge to surf the web, whose waves invariably took her to shores she did not long to walk upon. Then the coffee pot whistled and the phone rang. She looked at the clock. 8:47 a.m. Who in New York would dare call before nine? She grabbed her phone en route to the kitchen, flipped it on, and said "Hello" into a sea of static. Lower Manhattan was the land of interference, both visible and invisible.

"Hi, Lucy?"

"Yeah?" She poured hot water over the last of her Blue Mountain blend, and sucked up the fragrance of Jamaica.

"Hi, it's me. Rosa."

"Rosa! Hey, sorry I didn't recognize your voice. Why are you calling at—what is it, six a.m. out there?"

"Nah, it's nearly seven, Luce. Gotta hit the trail early, know what I mean?"

"Right. The trail." She meant it literally. Rosa Luxemburg, one of her closest friends, had fled New York for Santa

Fe, New Mexico, that adobified antique boutique for trust fund mystics and New Age artistes. Rosa had fallen in love with a drop-out lawyer from California on a trek out west last summer, and now she was gone. Gone riding every day, formal English style, for that's what she'd loved to do when she wasn't throwing paint around her studio down the street: chase the foxes through the forests of Westchester and New Jersey on her horse. Only now it was Santa Fe. She'd traded in the foxes for coyotes, and the Broome Street studio for the lawyer with a little house in the high desert. He played and taught golf and wanted to write, like everybody else. Rosa rode horses and made art, cruising on cash her father had made in plumbing fixtures. Her grandparents had been Commies of the Trotskyite persuasion, but then, so had lots of Lower East Side grandparents back in the Red Old Days. Rosa, on the other hand, was rich. "So what's up, Rosita?" Lucy said, pouring coffee.

"Same old shit. Get up at dawn, ride through the desert, work in the studio. It's a tough life."

"Yeah, I bet," said Lucy, wandering back to the computer. "How's Darren?"

"Oh, he's fine," Rosa said. "I'm teaching him to ride, he's giving me golf lessons. The sex is great."

"Not surprising. You're still in the preliminary rounds." God, trust fund life was rough. But she did love the girl. "So how's your work coming along?"

"Not bad, Luce. I'm doing these cloud paintings on faded wood. Found objects. The desert's really inspiring. God, I am so glad I got out of there, I tell you. When you're in New York you think you can't ever leave, and then when you leave you can't imagine what took you so long. Know what I mean?"

"I'm glad you're working again, Rosa. You're a talented girl."

"Hey, thanks. Listen, I'm on to something I thought you might be interested in. How's business, anyway?"

"About the same as when you left. There isn't any."

"Good. I mean—not good, but you'll be happy to hear this. Look, Darren met this woman down here and she's got a couple of Precolombian artifacts from Mexico that she just obtained, and she's sending them with a courier up to this gallery on Madison Avenue. They're putting a catalogue together and they need someone to photograph the pieces in a rush. Darren thought you might need the work."

"Sounds good. Who do I call?" Lord have mercy, a job. "Do they have any money?"

"Let's just say you can charge a serious day rate. This stuff is extremely valuable."

"Like fifteen hundred?"

She paused. "That seems pretty steep, Luce. How about a thousand?"

"Sure, why not. It's not like I'm fighting off the clients."

"I don't care. I mean, you could charge them five thousand a day as far as I'm concerned," said Rosa, "except that the people that run the gallery are old friends of Darren's parents."

"Don't worry about it, Rosita," Lucy said. "Either way I could use the gig. So what's the place called?"

"The Desert Gallery. It's on Madison, not far from the Whitney. You know the territory. Uptown art chic. I don't have the number here but the lady you need to talk to is called Madeleine Rooney. She's majority owner and runs the place. Has the money. Husband's a Wall Street guy. Darren tells me she looks like she eats once a month. She's expecting your call. It's a rush, like I said. I think you'll probably be shooting tomorrow or the next day at the latest."

"Great. Thanks a lot, Rosa. I really need the work."

"Sure. And listen, this stuff is seriously pricey so don't be put off if she seems paranoid."

"Gotcha. She wants to skin-search me, fine."

"So how're things in New York? Finally warming up?"

"Are you kidding? They say it's gonna hit eighty today. From winter to summer with an hour of spring."

"Typical. Only now you can attribute it to global warming and not just shitty New York weather, huh?"

"I guess." Lucy sighed. "You know, Rosita, I can't believe you're actually gone. I walk past your building and want to cry sometimes. All my friends are cutting out, and I feel so stuck."

"Come here."

"And what, live with you and Darren? I can't afford to live there, Rosie, you know that. There's no work."

"So how are you and Harry doing, anyway?"

"Ipswich? Fine, fine. He's—hell, why should I lie to you?" Lucy sighed. "We were doing great, and then he started drinking."

"Drinking? I thought he was a narc."

"He is, sort of, part time. But alcohol isn't illegal, though maybe it should be." She pictured her father, immobilized in his chair, bitterly drunk. "I guess Harry's more troubled about his brother than he likes to let on."

"The one who died?"

"OD'ed. Yeah. He gets on his high horse about dope, and then goes out and gets polluted on vodka and acts like its perfectly okay."

Rosa paused. "What a drag."

"No shit. So anyway, I told him I didn't want to see him for a while." Lucy typed "Harold Ipswich" onto her screen, deleted it, then undeleted it. She stared at the name. "So how is it, not being in New York, Rosa?"

"Well, like I said, it's great not having to put on your armor every time you go outside, but there's an edge in New York. I miss it. People are nice here, but . . . "

"Nice is not enough."

"Exactly. Still, no real regrets. The desert is so beautiful, you just can't imagine."

"Yeah, I bet. Well, listen, I better get on the phone with Madeleine Rooney, and then I gotta line up an assistant, and—"

"Oh, by the way, before you call her—I think she needs someone to write text on the pieces for the catalogue as well. You know anyone who might be interested?"

"Definitely. Beth and Quentin Washington. Remember them?"

"Your friends at the Indian museum, right?"

"Yeah. The next ones to leave Manhattan. Hannah's almost five and Beth's halfway to having another one, so they're ready to blow. But they know everything about Precolombian art, and they always need extra cash. I'll call them."

"Sounds good. Let me know how the shoot goes."

"Cool. Give my love to Darren."

"Right. And one of these days maybe you guys will meet and you'll see what I'm talking about."

"I sure hope so. Catch you later, Rosa."

"'Bye."

Lucy wandered into the kitchen to replenish her coffee, then threw open a window. The traffic roar got instantly louder. She leaned out and looked up and down Broadway.

Just 9:00 and already sticky hot. To the north the neo-Gothic spire of the Chrysler Building sparkled in the morning sun, and a steady stream of slow-moving cars flowed down Broadway. To the south, the Woolworth Building loomed. Five floors below, she watched her downstairs neighbor, Jane Aronstein, emerge from the building with Ross, her Labrador. The landlord popped out of his office next door a second later, in his silver-haired, weasel-like fashion, and he and Jane met on the sidewalk. Within seconds they were arguing. The elevator was probably stuck again.

Lucy pulled the window shut, went back to her desk, picked up the phone, and punched in a number.

"Museum."

"Hi. Quentin Washington, please."

"He's at the Brooklyn Annex."

"Then Beth."

"Just a minute." On hold, Lucy squeezed the phone between shoulder and ear and riffled through the phone book hunting a listing for the Desert Gallery, while her emissary roamed the dusty catacombs of the American Aboriginal Museum in search of Beth Washington.

Her incoming call signal beeped. "Damn." She switched over. "Hello. Lucy Ripken. Cherokee Productions," she added quickly.

"Hi, Lucy," came a monotone voice. "That was real professional-like. Could have fooled me."

"Who's this?"

"Simon. Simon Stevens. How's it going?"

"Simon, hey. I'm on another call, but I'm glad you called. Are you busy tomorrow?"

"Well, no, but I—"

"You want to work?"

"Yeah, I guess. What's the deal?"

"I'll call you back in ten minutes. Be there." She switched to the other line. "Hello."

"Hello?"

"Hi. Beth?"

"Yeah. Lucy! Hey, how're you doing?"

"Okay. How's it going up there? You busy?"

"Me? I'm just doing my computer thing, you know, cataloguing away. But Quentin's going nuts, they've got him—oh, never mind, you know how he is."

"The boy is tense. So how's Hannah?"

"Fine. Except that yesterday, after four months of discussion, she decided she didn't want a kid brother or sister after all."

"How nice for you."

"She'll just have to—it'll be fine. I just hope this Vermont thing works out. One kid in Manhattan is manageable. Two, I don't know."

"Any word on the Vermont gig?" Quentin was shortlisted for a job curating a small Revolutionary War museum near Bennington. If he got it they were gone, from the Big City to green New England.

"They're supposed to call next week. We're told it's a done deal, but who knows?"

"Meanwhile, I've got something interesting happening. Remember Rosa, my pal that moved to Santa Fe?"

"Yeah. How does she like it down there?"

"Fine, fine. But listen." Lucy gave Beth a shorthand version of the artifacts deal.

"Sounds intriguing," said Beth when Lucy had finished.

"That's why I called, Bethy. It's a major rush, and along with your knowledge I might need some help in setting up the shots. I don't know a thing about this stuff and I don't want to miss the point, photographically speaking. It's supposed to arrive at the Desert Gallery tomorrow morning."

"The Desert Gallery! You mean that Rooney woman's in on the deal?"

"You've heard of Madeleine Rooney?"

"Sure. Everybody in this business has. She's the unholy terror of the Precolombian art scene. God, I don't know if Quentin's going to want to get involved with her around."

"Come on. She can't be that bad."

"I shouldn't talk so much. You'll have to see for yourself. What time are you going there?"

"You can't leave me hanging like that, Beth. Please! What's the skinny on Madeleine Rooney?"

"Oh, nothing. She's just exactly what you'd expect from an Upper East Side lady running a Native American art gallery."

"Meaning?"

"She acts like she knows everything, she doesn't give a flying fuck about the work, she buys cheap and sells high. Does it all with the most fine-tuned gall you'll ever see."

"Sounds like fun."

"What can I say? Get your money as fast as you can. Expenses upfront if possible."

"Not likely. But Rosa's fiancé is a family friend, so I figure I won't get burned."

"Hmmm. I hope you're right. So what time tomorrow? Can we come at lunch?"

"I assume the stuff will be there by ten. We'll have to unpack and start setting up, so lunchtime should be about right. It's at Madison and—"

"We've been there," Beth interrupted.

"Oh. Okay. See you tomorrow. Regards to Quent and Hannah."

"Yeah. Twelve-thirtyish, depending on the trains."

Next she called the Desert Gallery. As she'd hoped, a machine answered. She identified herself, said she was planning to come up early tomorrow to shoot the pieces, and left her number for a callback to discuss deadlines and fees. She hung up and called Simon back. Simon wasn't a great assistant, but he was a big, handsome twenty-six-year-old kid and very charming. He'd be helpful with the Rooney woman, Lucy figured. He promised to be over at eight in the morning to help load the equipment into the car. Finally, Lucy called the HoSo Car Service, and after bantering with Ari the bad boy Israeli office manager and number one driver for a minute she lined up a car for the next morning. Once that was done she dressed and headed out in search of the *Times* and a little distraction. Which came in the form of a check in the mailbox, for nine hundred and seventy-three dollars, for a job she'd shot almost four months back. Saved! She walked down Broadway to the bank on Canal Street, practiced her Spanish with the multi-lingual ATM, then headed up Wooster to read the paper over a decaf double espresso at the Dean & DeLuca coffee bar. A check and a job. Things were definitely looking up.

Lucy and Simon sat in the backseat of a ruby-red, late-model, high-end Chrysler with white fake leather upholstery, cruising up Madison Avenue. "There," she said. "On the right. Behind that Checker cab." She did a quick fix with her lipstick as Ari swerved across two lanes of traffic to whip into the only available curb space, in front of a fire hydrant. "Simon, can you please unload while I go in and let her know we're here?" As she climbed out of the car, ran a hand through her hair, and approached the glass double doors of the Desert Gallery, Lucy felt mildly frazzled and anxious. To be expected. The Manhattan air was nearly visible, thick and hot at 8:45 a.m. in late April. Her dry cleaning hadn't been ready yesterday afternoon, and her black jumpsuit was better suited for fifty-degree weather. Inside the doors waited Madeleine Rooney. Lucy had left Rooney her message and gotten one back in return, in which the woman's hoarse, smudgy voice had okayed the shoot for today and suggested they talk fees and deadlines upon arrival. Lucy hated to make such a commitment—assistant, car, gear, haul uptown—without money matters settled, but having gotten the gig through a friend, she'd decided to play it by ear.

She tried the glass door, found it locked, and hit the bell, peering in. A long, elegant space, spotlit three-dimensional art on pedestals and stands. A wraith—a woman—rose up behind the counter in the back, and a second later the door buzzed softly. Lucy grabbed a handle and pulled it open.

She did a quick take on the room and liked what she saw. The Desert was austerely minimal in the manner of most galleries, but with a Santa Fe twist. The walls had rounded, adobe-style corners, and the paint was a shade of off-white most likely called Pueblo Pink or something along those lines. The floor was flagstone, the display stands were made of unfinished timbers, the display niches were rough-cut arches in the walls, and a couple of perfectly placed, dramatically spotlit Western accessories—an old saddle, a weathered Navajo blanket, and a ten-gallon hat with a bullet hole in the crown—instantly established the southwestern ambience, Ralph Lauren with a Native American twist. Counterpointing the southwestern mood, and elegantly stating the gallery's New York credentials, rows of high-tech tracklights sparkled in the ceiling, each focused precisely on a piece of art.

Also very New York in style was the gaunt, late-fiftyish woman coming toward Lucy from the back of the room.

She wore a black silk shirt gold-belted over black leggings on a scarecrow frame. Her expensively punk-styled blue-black hair framed a narrow oval face made lovelier, or at least less timeworn, by what appeared to be a well-executed facelift or two. Her diamonds—on ears, throat, hands—subtly sparkled and sang "Oh, how I have money, and I like it." She said, "Hello. I'm Madeleine Rooney." Again, that deep, hoarse voice. The Madeleine Rooney package was five feet tall, chic, sleek, and trendy to a slightly alarming degree.

"Lucy Ripken," Lucy said, and held out a hand. "How are you? What a great-looking space!"

"Thanks. I just had it re-done over the winter," Ms. Rooney said, and gave Lucy's hand a quick shake. Her fingers were cool and soft. "The courier dropped off the package a few minutes ago. I was just getting ready to unpack it. Where's your camera?"

"Outside in the car with my assistant. I thought we could talk fees first."

"Fine," she said, turning and walking away. "Is twelve hundred a day plus expenses suitable?" She tossed the words over her shoulder. "I'm assuming of course that you can do the whole job today. This is a rush."

"That's fine," Lucy said, pleased. Two hundred bucks more than she'd figured. "Expenses, including assistant, film, rush processing, the car, and miscellaneous stuff, will probably run another five hundred," she added, as Rooney dragged a small wooden shipping crate out from behind the slate-topped counter.

"I need film tomorrow. Can you get it done?" she said.

"No problem. And I've lined up a writer—two of them, actually. A husband and wife team. They'll be coming over at lunch. They work at the Aboriginal Museum and they know their stuff."

"Fine. You seem to have it under control. Darren said you were good."

"You talked to him today?"

"A few days ago. My regular photographer is in Vienna, and I simply must have this catalogue material at the printers the day after tomorrow."

"Well, you'll have film tomorrow, and I'm sure Quentin and Beth can turn around copy for you in no time."

"The Washingtons?" Rooney asked, and then, incongruously in the age of NO SMOKING, she placed a brown filterless European cigarette in her mouth and lit it with an elegant little solid gold lighter. She sucked in some smoke and coughed in a practiced manner.

"You know them?" Lucy asked.

"Of course. There aren't that many Precolombian experts in Manhattan, after all," she croaked. "I'm keeping the gallery closed today but I've invited a few special buyers in for a preview, so you'll have to work around them. Give me a hand with this, would you?" Rooney added, or rather demanded. Lucy whirled at the tone, ready to bite back. She bit her lip instead. Now that they'd agreed on money, Rooney had abandoned her efforts at politesse and assumed the role to which she was accustomed: boss.

"Sure." Lucy joined the woman in her cloud of imported toxins. "My driver's parked in front of a hydrant, but—"

"He can wait," Madame Rooney said, wielding a short crowbar. "You hold the crate steady, while I pry open the top." Lucy did as she was told. Madeleine Rooney quickly worked the top loose, then lifted it off to reveal a heap of styro peanuts. She plunged a hand in, pulled out an object buried in layers of plastic bubble wrap and tape, and began to unwrap it. A moment later, the first artifact was revealed. "Isn't it magnificent?" Rooney asked, holding up the object, a surprisingly naturalistic ceramic statue, about six inches high, of a young woman in an elaborate headdress and a robe embracing an older man, also robed. The faces were vaguely Asiatic. The door buzzed. They looked up. Simon Stevens's hulking silhouette loomed behind the glass. "Who's that?" Rooney snapped.

"My assistant," Lucy said. "Can you let him in?"

"Yes. But he does understand how delicate and valuable these pieces are, I assume," Rooney said, then went over and held down a button behind the counter. Simon stuck his head in the door.

"I'm all unloaded and the driver wants to split," he said. "I haven't got that much cash."

"Come on in," Lucy said. "Why don't you help Ms. Rooney for a minute? I'll take care of Ari. And close the door quickly. This stuff is very valuable." Simon strolled back, and Lucy could feel Madeleine loosening up, transforming herself into the coquette as she got a better look at the big, handsome boy. He was six-two, one-eighty, with jet-black hair and blue eyes. He could pass for a model, and still wasn't sure if he wanted to take pictures or be in them. "Simon, this is Mrs. Rooney," she said.

"Call me Madeleine," Rooney said, offering him a smile, the first Lucy had seen, and a hand. He shook it.

"Hi," he grinned, entirely at ease. "Simon Stevens. Nice to meet you. Great-looking gallery you've got here," he added, glancing around. "Wow, isn't that a Jaina Island ceramic?" he asked, noticing the object she was holding.

"Simon, I didn't know you knew Precolombian art," Lucy said.

"Surprise, surprise. I majored in art history, Lucy," he said. "Did two semesters on Precolombian. This is from the Yucatán—Late Classic period of the Maya. The moon goddess embracing an older deity, right, Madeleine?"

"My, you do know your stuff," said Madeleine, injecting a coy tone into her vocal rasp. "I wouldn't have known it if you hadn't told me, Simon."

"I'm going to take care of Ari," Lucy said. "Back in a minute. And you've got to help me bring the gear in, Si, so don't get too relaxed just yet." Simon preferred bullshitting around with clients to working. He was good at it— bullshitting around with clients—but that was only part of what she hired him to do.

Lucy paid Ari, adding a big tip for making him wait— got to keep guys like him on your side—and then she and Simon hauled the gear in the front door.

After some discussion and a look through a couple of art books and catalogues for comparison, Rooney decided she wanted 4 x 5-inch transparencies of the pieces. Lucy couldn't fault her for that, the large format film did look much better, but it meant she had a bit more work to do. They set up a display pedestal, and then Lucy broke out the bellows-style camera and began to assemble it while Simon rigged the lights. By the time they were ready to shoot the first one Madeleine Rooney had the crate unpacked, and had lined up the pieces on the slate countertop in a neat row—several hundred thousand dollars' worth of ceramic and carved objects, all Late Classic Mayan in derivation. There was a second two-figure statue, a variation on the first with slightly different versions of the same pair of deities embracing. Traces of yellow pigment added luster to this second piece. There were two shell objects, one of a man riding on the back of a sea monster of a sort, the other of a young woman whom Simon identified as Ixchell, the fertility goddess. The carved iconographic detail was intricate and extraordinary. There was a single carved obsidian object, a head in profile that probably had decorated the top of a scepter or sword, also highly detailed with iconography; and finally there was the most precious object of all, a complete, unblemished cylindrical vase, with polychromatic paint illustrations, in almost perfect condition, depicting a range of activities and beings— human, supernatural, and animal—in strikingly dramatic fashion. The imagery on the pot, at first confusing to look at, after a while sorted itself out, and the narrative action became evident. It was an amazing illustration of a world view from a lost time and place, the Mayan civilization of the Yucatán. Lucy was awed by it, even as she contemplated photographing it. The pot would require several photographs to show all the sides. According to Madeleine Rooney, it was worth somewhere between two hundred thousand and five hundred thousand dollars, depending,

Lucy supposed, on how the Dow did that week. Handle with care was an understatement.

They had shot several digital test shots, adjusted the lights, loaded a sheet of film, and were ready to make the first exposure when the buzzer sounded again at a little past noon. Rooney let Quentin and Beth Washington in the door.

"Luce," said Quentin, striding over to hug her. "How are you doing?" He was temperamental and somewhat delicate, tall, thin, high-waisted, high-strung, and long-legged, crane-like, with a large nose, curly hair, and a wide forehead over pale green eyes. He came from New England blueblood, complete with a DAR grandma. He had dressed, as usual, in slim-fitting jeans and a blue workshirt.

"Not bad," Lucy said. "Hey, Beth," she added, with a quick hug for Quentin's wife. Beth was five years younger than Lucy and Quentin. She was a solid, brilliant, handsome, brown-haired Jewish woman who came from Lower East Side radical stock like Rosa, except her parents had only made it as far north as Yonkers. Her father still practiced leftist law, and was not rich. Beth and Quentin were an odd yet perfectly suited New York couple. "You guys know Mrs. Rooney," Lucy said, deferring to the money.

"Hi," said Beth. "How are you?" The gallery queen nodded recognition.

"Hello, Madeleine," Quentin said offhandedly, glancing at Rooney, his tone perfectly arch. "How are you? My God," he interrupted himself as he spotted the artifacts lined up on the counter. "Look at this! Beth, can you believe it! It's from Jaina! Fantastic! Where did you find these?" He approached the pieces, more fired up than Lucy had seen him since they all gave up recreational drugs. "Do you mind if I have a closer look at this?" He looked at Madeleine Rooney.

She nodded. "I don't have to tell you to be careful, do I, Quentin?" she said.

"No." He laughed. "I would hate to have to sell my daughter in order to pay for breaking one of these." He gently picked up the conch carving of the man on the sea monster and carried it over into the brighter light under a row of ceiling tracks. The doorbell sounded, and after taking a good look Madeleine Rooney buzzed in a client, then headed up to the door for personal greetings and an apology for the chaos in the gallery. Lucy heard her begin to crow at Mrs. Hopkins—or Agnes, as Rooney gushingly called the lady—about the new pieces. Agnes Hopkins carried a sleek black shopping bag in one hand and had tucked a small terrier under the other arm. Madeleine Rooney greeted the animal, named Duncan, with nearly as much enthusiasm as she had greeted its owner. The dog emitted high-pitched yaps and resentful little growls from its position under the lady's arm.

"Beth, have you met Simon Stevens, my photo assistant?" Lucy asked, tuning ladies and dog out. "Simon, Beth Washington."

"Hi," said Simon, "How ya doin'?"

"Beth, come here a minute," said Quentin impatiently.

"Hi." Beth shook Simon's hand quickly. "Excuse me, Quentin gets so excited about this stuff."

"Go on," said Lucy. "Have a better look." She watched with amusement, and perhaps a touch of envy, as Quentin and Beth huddled over the little shell figure, passing a magnifying glass back and forth. Lucy had thought the piece unquestionably lovely, but it didn't have the mysterious potency for her that it did for them. They knew where it came from, what it meant, who had created it and why, and knowing this made all the difference.

Ms. Rooney waltzed back with Agnes Hopkins to show her the goods. "Pardon the mess," Rooney said as she walked past, "I simply had to have this photography done today to get the catalogue printed on schedule, you see, dear?"

"Oh, don't worry, Maddy," said Agnes, rail-thin and elegaunt, just like Madeleine, as she eyeballed Simon. "I know how it is. I've been re-decorating like mad, and there are workmen stomping around my house constantly." She passed Lucy without so much as a nod to indicate that she recognized her existence, although the terrier snapped fiercely in Lucy's direction. Lucy threw her black cloth over her head and gazed through the camera.

Quentin called softly, "Hey, Luce." She popped out from under the cloth and glanced at him. He waved her over, watching Rooney surreptitiously. Rooney and her client were too engrossed in admiring the goods on the counter to notice.

Lucy said, "Si, see if you can discover from Ms. Rooney where we can get some lunch." Then she joined Beth and Quentin in the corner. "What's up?" she asked.

"Lucy, where did she get this stuff?" Quentin asked, waving the small carving in the air.

"I don't know. I didn't ask."

"They're fakes," Quentin said quietly. "At least this one is, and I'd be willing to bet they all are."

"What?" Lucy snapped sharply. "But Simon said that—"

"Really well executed," Beth said, "but definitely forged."

"How can you tell? How do you know?"

"Look," Quentin said, holding up the piece. "See this?" he held the magnifying glass up to the figurine. "See these markings along the bottom of the fishy creature? These kinds of patterns aren't—they don't belong on a piece like this. This is what forgers do a lot of the time—take imagery off something they know, in this case, ceramic figurines, and re-create it somewhere else. But this pattern was never used in shell carvings. Least not that I've seen, and I think I've seen most everything around. No way this thing wasn't made in the last year or so."

"Jesus," said Lucy, her heart sinking. There went the job. She had a flash of inspiration, but it died even as the words came out. "Can you wait till I finish shooting them to—"

"Come on, Lucy," Quentin said. "We can't do that. She might be selling one to that dame right now," he said, glowering at the two women over by the counter.

"Yeah, you're right," she said. "Damn. Well, you want to do the talking, Quentin? I know I don't."

"Sure. Let's get it over with." He led the way to the counter, where Duncan greeted them with a renewed burst of yapping. "Um, excuse me, Madeleine."

"You want to talk fees, Quentin? Fine. Would you mind waiting a few moments? Can't you see I'm busy?"

"No, I don't want to talk fees, Ms. Rooney. I want to talk about the pieces. Privately, if it's all right."

His tone caught her attention. "Excuse me, Agnes," she said. "I'll just be a moment. Let's go into my office, Quentin. Don't let Dunkie peepee on the floor, now, Agnes."

"Now don't you worry," Agnes said. "Dunkie's a good little boy, isn't he?" she said, lapsing into babytalk and stroking her dog. Lucy followed the Washingtons and Madeleine Rooney through a door behind the counter into her office. Prints, posters, and pieces of art were scattered about the glass-topped desk in the middle of the room. Lucy closed the door. The three of them faced Rooney.

"What is it, Quentin?" said Madeleine Rooney, anxiety surfacing in her voice. "Is there a problem?"

"Well, yes," said Quentin, placing the little carving on the desk. "This." He picked it up again. "See this?" he said, indicating the iconography on the sea monster. "This doesn't belong here, Madeleine."

"What do you mean, 'doesn't belong'?"

"This iconography is ripped off a ceramic piece. I don't know exactly which one, but—"

"What do you mean, 'ripped off'?"

"This is a fake, Madeleine," he said, not without some satisfaction. "I know Mayan work, and they never put these patterns on shell carvings."

"What are you talking about?" she said, snatching it away from him. "I have papers. These pieces were certified by a man in Santa Fe. I can't remember his name, but he was—Margaret Clements said—" She drew herself up. "I'm afraid you're mistaken. I have letters of authentication."

"I'll be happy to look at them," said Quentin. "But that doesn't change the fact that this piece is bogus. I think we'd be wise to check the others before you show them to anybody else, although I doubt that any of them are authentic.

Why would a forger put anything real in with a bunch of fakes?"

"Wait here a moment," Rooney said, and bustled out of the office.

"Well, that could have been worse," Beth said.

"So much for my gig," Lucy said. "I can't imagine she's going to want this stuff photographed if it isn't what it's supposed to be."

They watched through the window as Rooney talked Agnes Hopkins and her dog toward the front door. "Sorry, Lucy," said Quentin. "Way it goes. Well, that bitch is out the door. Let's go check out the other pieces."

He led the way back into the gallery, where they joined Madeleine Rooney and Simon by the counter with its row of artifacts. Quentin picked another shell carving and examined it with his magnifying glass. "Yes, like I thought. Same deal. Another fake."

"I don't know what makes you so sure these are fake," said Simon. "I studied this stuff in school, and I'm not so certain."

"Forget it, Simon," said Lucy. "Quentin knows more about this stuff than you could ever comprehend."

"Now, wait a minute," said Rooney. "Maybe Simon has a point. Maybe you're making a mistake, Quentin."

Quentin looked exasperated. "Get serious, Madeleine. Do you think I would dare to screw up a call as important as this? No way. Simon, I'm sure you know your stuff, but you have no idea how good these forgers have gotten in the last couple of years. As the market for these pieces has grown, and the prices have climbed, a higher quality of hustler has jumped in. These dudes are experts. Believe me, if I hadn't seen it before, I wouldn't have known what to look for. Madeleine, you're wasting your time pretending otherwise."

"I'm not so sure. I want to talk to—I want Herman Forte to have a look."

"Forte?" said Quentin. "You're going to call Herman Forte? There's nothing he's going to tell you that I haven't already."

"There's too much at stake here. I simply must speak to someone with more authority," she said, and went back to her office. She closed the door.

"Who's Herman Forte?" Lucy asked.

"Dr. Herman Forte," said Beth. "He used to be our boss. A real classic New York academic shithead. But he's a Ph.D., and he loves ladies like Madeleine Rooney."

"Christ, I can't believe she's calling him," said Quentin. "Thanks for raising those doubts, Simon," he said. "Perhaps you'd like to come back to the museum with me and tell me how to do my job there as well?" He stopped abruptly, and turned his attention back to the objects, peering closely at the vase. "This one would have to be subjected to thermo-luminescence to date it, but like I said before, I've never heard of anyone trying to pass off forgeries and real artifacts at the same time. I'd be willing to bet this is bogus, too."

"I'm sorry, Quentin," Simon said. "I was just trying to help."

"Don't make excuses. You fucked up, Si," said Lucy. "And where's lunch, anyway, you galoot?"

"There's a deli around the corner. What do you guys want?" he said sheepishly.

Rooney emerged from her office. "Herman's on his way over. Meanwhile, I'd like you to continue shooting, Lucy. I want these pieces in the catalogue."

"Really?" Lucy said, her spirits instantly lifted. Fake or no, what did she care, if the lady still wanted pictures?

"Yes. Let's get on with it." Rooney picked up one of the shell carvings and placed it on the pedestal. "I'll just have to find someone else to write them up if you two aren't interested."

Quentin and Beth just looked at her. Quentin shook his head.

"I was just going to get some sandwiches," Simon said to Rooney. "Do you want anything?"

"I never eat lunch," she said. "But fetch me a bottle of Evian, Simon. Thanks."

"I'll have a Greek salad–type thing," said Lucy. "You know, feta, olives, yogurt, and cucumbers."

"Don't bother with us," said Quentin. "We've got to get back to work, right, Beth?" He glanced at his watch, an expression of contempt on his face.

"Right, Quentin."

"See ya, Luce," Quentin said. "Sorry," he added under his breath, "but this is total bullshit—and the last person I want to see right now is Herman Forte."

"That's cool, Quent, but she still wants her pics," she said.

"Go for it, Luce," he said. "A picture of a fake is just as pretty as a picture of an artifact."

"Let us know what Forte says, Lucy," Beth said. "Talk to you tonight. Ciao, Ms. Rooney," she added from the doorway, and waved as she sailed out.

Herman Forte showed up just as Lucy and Simon were finishing up their lunch. Forte was crew-cut and a boyish fifty, dressed snappily in a lightweight suit over a blue striped shirt and a bow tie. "Madeleine, how are you?" he gushed as they rushed to meet mid-room. They hugged and continental kissed and did their dance, then cut to the chase: the artifacts.

Madeleine Rooney took him by the arm and led him over to the counter, babbling all the while: "So Quentin Washington claims these are fakes but I don't know, this nice boy Simon says he doesn't think so, and I have papers, and I don't know; Herman, I can't believe Darren would let Maggie Clements send up a bunch of forgeries, do you?"

"Certainly seems unlikely to me," he said, picking up the obsidian head and looking it over. "Hmmmm. What did Quentin actually say, Madeleine?"

"Oh, something about the iconography along the bottom—who cares about the bottom, for God's sake?— belonging on ceramics and not on shell or stone pieces. Frankly, I don't see how anyone could know with such certainty that the Mayans didn't use the same patterns on different media," she said.

Forte looked at the iconography more carefully, then put it down and picked up one of the shell pieces and checked it out before setting it down. "Um, I don't know, Madeleine. I just don't know. Quentin may be right, I can't be sure. On the other hand," he added quickly, seeing her dismay, "He may be wrong. I'm not convinced either way, to tell the truth." He simply couldn't stand the idea of displeasing the lady.

"Herman," Madeleine whined, "Herman, what do you really think?"

"I think you should definitely go ahead with the photography and the catalogue. I'll have to think about it. Maybe I can get Louis Schultz to have a look."

"So they aren't fake? Washington was wrong?" she cried out.

"Now, now," he said, pleased to have pleased her, "I didn't say that. I said simply that there was some doubt. I'm not sure. I could go either way with this one. I think we need another opinion. I'll have to see what—"

"Fine. Lucy, we'll definitely finish up the shoot. Herman, do you have time to write these up for the catalogue?"

"I might be able to manage. It would have to be a rush, of course, with attendant fees. And I'd like to see the letters of authentication, if I could, Madeleine. I need to know who's seen the pieces."

"In my office. Come on back and have a look. Call your friend. Do whatever you have to." Madeleine could hardly contain her re-kindled excitement. And who could blame her, Lucy thought.

But on the other hand, how was this sycophantic snivel-worm going to pull this off? Lucy wondered. If he was legit and the pieces weren't, he was putting his reputation on the line by authenticating them. Could Quentin have been wrong? No way. He was one of the smartest people she knew, and this was his work. He would never fuck up a call this important.

Well, for now, it was not her problem. "Well, Simon, I guess we oughta get to it, eh?" she said.

"Yeah. Hey, Luce," he added. "I'm sorry about what happened before, but—hey, maybe your friend was wrong, huh?"

"Not likely, Si, not likely. Let's just get the job done, eh? I don't want to hang around here any longer than necessary."

2

A Frolic in the High Desert

Lucy sweated the take-off, the only part of flying that occasionally rattled her nerves, and then settled down as the jet lifted smoothly through the east coast cloud cover and swooped west, Albuquerque bound. Before getting into the *Times* for her daily dose of domestic and international disaster, to re-affirm her phenomenal stroke of luck she opened the assignment letter for another look.

The letterhead read *NY/See Style*, done up in a hot red deconstructivist typeface. Heidi Landesmann, Editor. Phone and fax numbers and a website and a Lafayette Street address. Heidi was an old friend from Lucy's club-crawling days who'd stumbled into a low-paying East Village edit job five years back, inadvertently hitching a ride on the fastest rising star in the New York City magazine firmament. Now the star was on the verge of imploding, though Heidi reported that the publishers hoped to squeak through the current hard times and flourish again, possibly by closing the magazine's ill-fated online edition. Lucy had her doubts. But *NY/See Style* still had an editorial budget, and in the latest shake-up of the masthead Heidi had been anointed editor-in-chief, opening the door for Lucy at last.

Dear Lucy Ripken:

This is to confirm an assignment on Precolombian art forgery and its relationship to and effect on the N.Y. art market. The article will specifically focus on works from the Mayan culture of Precolombian Mexico. As agreed, NY/See Style will pay $1500.00 on delivery of a 3000- to 5000-word manuscript on the subject. NY/SS will pay an additional $500.00 for photography, and $150.00 for each image utilized in the article. NY/SS agrees to pay all photography expenses; round-trip airfare to Albuquerque, New Mexico; car rental; and research expenses, excluding hotel and food bills. Good luck.

Heidi Landesmann

There was a yellow stick-on note attached. "Luce—like I said off the record: You get the right picture, you got the cover and another $1000. Love to Rosa. Stay cool. H." Lucy put the letter away and looked out the window. The clouds had parted to reveal green rippling hills seven miles below. She wondered about her own dumb luck. One minute she's doing a basic one-day photo shoot to make rent, the next she's on her way to Santa Fe with a hot investigative assignment and a shot at a cover story. This could be a major career break, no doubt about it. So what if she had to crash with Rosa and Darren, and eat on the cheap? There might even be a book in this story—one that she would write with a little help from her friends Beth and Quentin Washington.

After all, she'd hatched the idea over dinner at their house right after the photo shoot. They were dying to get the details on what Forte had said about the fake goods, and so Lucy had dropped Simon and her photo gear off downtown and headed right back uptown on the train, this time all the way to 199th and Broadway, where Quentin, Beth, and Hannah lived in the shadow of the Cloisters.

Over brown rice, black beans, Caesar salad, and Mexican beer, Lucy'd gained a little more insight into the current Precolombian art scene as well as some background on Dr. Herman Forte, an "obsequious swine," Beth had called him. By the end of dinner Lucy had come up with a plan for an investigative article on the Precolombian art market, and the production and distribution of fakes, particularly those purporting to be Mayan relics from the Yucatán Peninsula, into that market. As was true of much that was written on art these days, the story would really be about money. Beth and Quentin had agreed to "consult."

She started making calls the next morning. *The Smithsonian* and *Connoisseur* wanted elaborate written queries, while *Art in America*, *Traveler*, and *Art & Antiques* turned her down flat. Then she thought of Heidi L., and just like that landed the gig.

A piece of good timing, as *NY/See Style* was in the midst of another facelift, the third in two years, and its editorial policies were in flux. This meant that Heidi could give Lucy a real assignment on a subject the rag wouldn't have touched a few years back. In the loud and lavish recent past, *NY/SS* had been all fashion, so trendy it practically disintegrated in your hands when you tried to get past the self-consciously grainy black and white neo-brutalist fashion pics and read the text. The articles and columns consisted of innuendo and in-the-know chat about who showed up at the latest club, what they wore, and what drugs they took while there. It was fitting, since the magazine had begun as an amateur nightlife gazette run by a bunch of aging club kids who thought what they did every evening from midnight to dawn merited press coverage. Lucy had hated *NY/SS* even though she'd devoured the nightlife gossip for the first year of its existence, to see if anyone she knew got boldfaced. They never did. She never did.

"A controversy about Precolombian art forgery?" Heidi had said. "Ridiculously pricey fake Mayan pots and statues? Sounds cool. Tell me more." Lucy did, and Heidi said, "Well, nobody around here knows what the magazine is about anymore, you could use the work, and I've got a few pages to fill, so why not?"

They ironed out the details. The article would open with the scene in the Desert Gallery. Good thing she'd closed the shoot with a color portrait of Rooney surrounded by the new pieces, their elongated and distorted shadows crawling up her arms and body. The first section would end with the arrival of Herman Forte to make his ambiguous endorsement. The tone in this part would be decidedly catty, as rich, dessicated Upper East Side art groupies like Madeleine Rooney and academic suck-ups like Herman Forte invariably played well as objects of ridicule. From there the piece would track back through Margaret Clements in Santa Fe and lead where it would. Trendy Santa Fe would make great background, and was a major center for dealing Native American art both contemporary and Precolombian. Lucy had three weeks to figure it out, shoot what she needed, and write the story.

She only wished she'd seen the letters of authentication and the appraisal that Madeleine Rooney insisted she'd gotten from New Mexico. These documents supported her claim that the stuff was authentic. Herman Forte had seen the documents, but Rooney had refused to let Lucy see them. She said it was none of her business. Lucy had returned the favor by not informing Rooney of her plans for an article on the controversy.

She read the *Times* from end to end, almost completed the puzzle, and then began skimming the book that Quentin had lent her. It was called *The Maya*, by George A. Coe. Quentin had called it the definitive volume.

It knocked her out. When she woke, the flight attendant was murmuring the passengers back to upright in their seats as the plane soared down into the desert. Light poured through the scratchy windows, and Lucy had a look out. The spring air was luminously clear over Albuquerque, and they landed smoothly ten minutes ahead of schedule.

When the plane stopped moving she quickly hauled her camera bag and her purse down from the overhead. She positioned one bag in front and one behind, readying herself for the daily backache, and with the straps crossing over her shoulders, she edged her way along with the men and women in suits down the aisle and out into the terminal.

Fifteen minutes later she left the airport in a cheap subcompact rental car, pleasantly surprised, once again, at how easily things like luggage, cars, and airport exits got done outside New York. She headed northeast on Interstate 25, up the Rio Grande toward Santa Fe. High on her right, morning shadows stretched down the western face of Sandia Peak.

Doing seventy-five miles an hour with all four windows down and the radio blasting rock n' roll, she recalled a more pleasurable scenario from a dozen years back, driving cross-country from Portland to the Big Apple. She and Billy Larson, the first guy she'd ever slept with, had a dozen Dexedrine, half an ounce of reefer, and four days to get a drive-away car—a late-model Lincoln—to a place called Hempstead on Long Island. Even with a side swoop into the desert they'd made it in seventy-six and a half high and hallucinatory hours. From Hempstead they'd taken the train back into Manhattan, where she'd fallen in love not with Billy, who became a junkie then went home to Oregon and got religion, but with the city itself, all speed, clamor, and glorious decay.

No decay out here. Desert and distant mountains glowed, pristine in the perfect light, the thin, rarefied air. Spring wildflowers splashed the muted beige tones of the earth with bright accents. The Sangre de Cristos showed off their gleaming faces and deep, shadowy arroyos. At the side of the road, three pink-headed vultures flapped up on heavy black wings as she blasted past, disturbed from a road-kill feast.

The fast-food, gas-station trash architecture that marks the outskirts of every U.S. town in the early twenty-first century had infested picturesque Santa Fe, too, once you got off the interstate. She exited and headed toward the Plaza, measuring the neon and plastic sprawl of shopping malls and gas stations against the looming mountains.

Closer to the Plaza, tasteful took over. Thanks to a five-story height restriction and other zoning controls inside the city limits, the streets were lined with low-rise adobe or faux adobe buildings, reducing everything—fancy hotel, department store, government office—to the same unpretentious if somewhat monochromatic level. Around the Plaza itself, where the Palace of the Governors and the other authentic seventeenth, eighteenth, and nineteenth-century pueblo buildings were located, the town was lovelier and more substantial. But some things had changed in three or four hundred years, and Lucy couldn't find a place to park anywhere near the Anasazi Mountain Lodge, where she was supposed to meet Rosa at one o'clock for lunch. She ended up in a lot three blocks away, and counted three jewelry stores, five arts and crafts emporiums, six art galleries displaying O'Keeffe and her clones and descendants, two western wear shops, and four nouvelle Tex-Mex restaurants in the three-block walk. Lucy strolled—or rather trudged, since she had her overstuffed camera bag slung over a shoulder—through a few of the shops and galleries, and discovered that ridiculously high prices had migrated west from Madison Avenue. Tastefully hip, gracefully aging, exquisitely accessorized men and women—the sort that looked as if they probably spent a lot of time in mud baths and channeling seminars—ran the elegant little stores. Outside, the streets teemed with whites in fancy casual western duds buying, and Native Americans selling silver and turquoise jewelry off blankets on the plaza sidewalks. Flowers bloomed everywhere in terra cotta pots. From certain angles the way the sunlight streaked the perfect adobe buildings made it look as if Ralph Lauren had designed the entire town.

She spotted the Lodge, familiar from photographs, from half a block away. She'd done a design story on the Anasazi a year or so back for *Spaces* magazine, and remembered the timbered entry arch and the heavy wooden doors from the photos she'd worked with when writing the piece.

She and Rosa had decided to meet here because it was the only place in town Lucy knew of, and Rosa had been looking for an excuse to come in for lunch. Darren, it seemed, simply refused to patronize places that charged more than five bucks for a taco, even if the tortilla was made from organic blue corn, the chicken had ranged free, and the beans were genetically pure and politically correct.

Lucy entered the lodge's restaurant and had a quick look around. The room was half-full, mostly groups of prosperous young white women doing lunch, but Rosa, the quintessential prosperous young white woman, was not among them. Lucy had traveled 1800 miles, Rosa had to travel three, and it was Rosa who would be late for lunch. Lucy checked her watch, which she'd set on landing in Albuquerque. She was four minutes late. It was not a good time to utilize her usual approach to late lunch dates, which was to give them ten minutes then leave. Where could she go? Shopping?

The hostess, an elegant Hispanic woman with OLGA stitched over the pocket of her tailored cowboy shirt, gave Lucy a practiced smile as she approached the maître d' stand. "Good afternoon. Will you be dining alone?"

"No, I'm meeting someone, but she's not here. The reservation is under Luxemburg, or maybe Ripken, I don't know."

Olga looked at her list. "Would that be Lucy Ripken?"

"That's me."

"I have a letter here for you," Olga said, handing Lucy an envelope.

"I can't believe it," Lucy said with a sigh, dropping her camera bag heavily. "I come across the country for lunch, and I get a note instead of a date."

"It's not from your lunch partner," said Olga. "It's from the owner of the hotel, Mr. Sobel. He was looking over the reservation list this morning, and when he saw your name he got very excited. He asked me to give you this."

"Yo, Luce," came a familiar voice, and Lucy whirled with excitement as Rosa dashed over. They met in a big hug.

"I can't believe it," Rosa said. "You look great. So fashionable!"

"Hey, I'm from New York, what can I say?" Lucy said. "But look at you! What's this, cowgirl chic?" Rosa wore faded jeans, a black shirt with a cowskull in white on the front, and black cowboy boots. "Jesus, look at those muscles." She grabbed Rosa's bicep. "You been wrangling steers, or what?"

"Four hours on horseback everyday'll do it to you," she said. Then she lowered her voice. "Can you believe it, I'm getting bowlegged from horses and sex, but my thighs are so big and muscular they rub together when I walk anyway." Lucy laughed, checking her out.

Rosa was a little shorter than Lucy's five foot eight, but built more solidly—all muscular legs, arms, and back, with a big firm chest. She had white skin with pale brown freckles, reddened now from the sun, dark green eyes, and thick black hair, cut medium long in back with bangs in front. Lucy thought her the most beautiful girl on earth, but that's because she was her best buddy. Though Rosa looked like Veronica to Lucy's Betty, they called themselves the Two Veronicas, since they both had her personality.

"So let's sit down and pig out," said Rosa. "I'm starved."

"Me too. I ordered a fruit plate for the plane, and it consisted of rotten strawberries and unripe cantaloupe."

"I hear the baby back ribs here are great," Rosa said.

"We're ready for a table now, Olga," Lucy said. She turned back to Rosa, and said, "Ribs? For lunch?" Rosa could eat twice her body weight every day and never gain an ounce. Intense exercise helped, but it was fundamentally a matter of genetics. She was simply built that way. Lucy, on the other hand, watched her weight constantly, swam a mile a day, did aerobics three times a week, and ate mostly salad. As a result she had a muscular butt but otherwise stayed slim. She would never put on muscle all over like Rosa did. Instead she put on fat, when she let her guard down.

Today was a day for sending the guard home, Lucy decided as Olga showed them to a table. They sat, picked up the menus, and put them down. "So," said Rosa. "We have a problem with the art."

"Yes. Well, not exactly a problem for me, since I got an assignment out of it," Lucy said. "But for Madeleine Rooney, a serious problem. Hey, let's forget about the art a minute, Rosita. Oh, I should read this," Lucy said, suddenly remembering the letter in her hand. Rosa looked curious. "It's from the hotel owner, this guy Robert Sobel," Lucy added. "The hostess had it when I got here. Remember I said I did a piece on the place? I interviewed him on the phone for it, and we had a pretty long chat. He's kind of a New Age philosopher/ entrepreneur type, you know?"

"Yeah. The town's full of them. They all want to make a lot of money without damaging the environment or exploiting labor. Which can't really be done," said Rosa, betraying her Commie roots. "So go ahead. I'll read the menu."

Lucy ripped the envelope open and pulled out the letter for a quick skim.

"Well, what do you know," she said. "Sobel wants to comp me."

"What do you mean?" Rosa said.

"He's offered me two nights free, and a couple of dinners, as a quote 'gesture of gratitude' for the article. Nice of him to make the offer."

"I thought you were going to stay with me and Darren, Luce."

"I'm going to be here at least a week, Rose. We'll have plenty of time to hang out. Meanwhile, I can't pass up a couple of free nights in the lap of luxury."

"You're right. I was just being selfish. Hey, forget it. Our house doesn't quite cut it for luxury, I have to say. But check out the menu. It sounds like Alan Watts or maybe Carlos Castaneda wrote it up."

They perused the poetic menu and ordered lunch from a waitress named Katrina, from Chicago, who was a Gemini with three planets in Leo. Then they ate massive quantities of great organic food. One of the many things that bound their friendship was a mutual love of food and mistrust of people who didn't like eating.

"Well," said Rosa, putting down her espresso cup and leaning back, an hour or so later, "now that we've achieved major bloatdom, and figured out what to do with Harry and Darren, give me the update on the Rooney situation."

"God, that was good, wasn't it?" Lucy tossed her napkin on the table. "Well, nothing's changed since we talked on the phone. I haven't seen the papers, Forte is waffling but sounds to me like he's leaning toward authenticating the stuff, and Quentin wants nothing to do with it."

"Will he raise a stink if Forte does what he has to and Rooney holds her auction?"

"Rosa, get real. There's no way this thing can work out that way. They're fakes, Rose. Nobody's going to buy them."

Rosa countered. "You should talk to Darren. He's been on the phone with Maddie—Madeleine—Rooney. Sorry, that's what he calls her. Anyway, she's called a couple of times. And now she wants to talk to you ASAP."

"You told her I was coming here?"

"Darren did, I think. Does it matter?"

"I don't know. Did you tell her why?"

"It may have come up. I don't remember."

"Well, a little discretion might have been useful."

"Lucy, come on. How could Darren or I know you hadn't told Madeleine you were planning to write about the pieces?"

"You're right, Rosita. But she's got a lot to lose when the truth comes out. As does your friend Clements. Has anyone talked to her?"

"We thought we'd wait for you to get here."

"Thanks. I appreciate that."

"More coffee, Miss Ripken?" Lucy looked up. A distinguished-looking man of about fifty, with silver hair pulled back into a short ponytail and an elegant little Confucian goatee, held a coffee pot over the table. He wore not a waiter's shirt but a tailored western-style suit and a string tie with a silver clasp. He smiled at Lucy.

Confused for an instant, she suddenly remembered him from a black and white picture she'd seen in a press kit. "Mr. Sobel!" she declared, and stood. "How are you? More to the point, what are you doing pouring coffee? Rosa, this is Robert Sobel, the man I told you about—the owner of the hotel. Mr. Sobel, this is my friend, Rosa Luxemburg. She moved here from New York last year."

"May I?" he said, putting the coffee pot down on the table and taking Lucy's hands for a two-handed shake and some serious eye contact. With his silver gray, smoky eyes, warmly tanned skin, and elegant diction, Lucy found him undeniably magnetic. "Lucy, so pleased to meet you at last. When I saw your name on the guest list I was just thrilled. I loved the piece. You captured our zeitgeist *con perfección*. Thanks so much. Hello, Ms. Luxemburg, lovely to see you." He shook Rosa's hand, then took Lucy's again. "So what do you think, Lucy, now that you're here, does our little hostel match up to your expectations? Photography can be very flattering."

"Oh, it's wonderful. Everything feels very authentic, and the lunch was great. But why are you pouring coffee?"

"Remember what I told you about our efforts at getting the community involved in the hotel, and vice versa? Well, one thing we like to do here is stay in touch with what our employees are experiencing. What better way than to get on the floor and work with them?" With that he finally let go of her hands.

"What a lovely concept," Lucy said. There was a pause. He smiled and held her eyes with his. "Well," Lucy said, a little unnerved by his unwavering gaze. Was he enlightened, was he horny, or was he a body that had been snatched, replaced by an entrepreneurial pod from the New Age? "Would you care to join us for coffee?"

"I would, but I'm working," he answered. "Just a moment, ma'am," he said to an irritated-looking woman waving at him from the next table. "I'll be right there." He picked up the coffeepot. "We've given you the Laredo Suite," he said. "It's one of the big ones." He moved away, coffee pot poised.

"Well," said Rosa when he was out of range. "Do you think the working class song and dance was entirely for our—I should say your—benefit, or what?"

"I don't think so," Lucy said. "I don't know how he made his first million, but I think his intentions are good these days. He's making a real effort."

"Yeah, yeah, well, do you think he lets that guy"—she nodded at a Mexican busboy standing in the kitchen doorway—"make management decisions when it's his turn to play boss?"

"Hey, come on, give him a break. For a rich guy he's all right." Funny, her saying that to Rosa, with her fat trust fund. Besides, why did she feel protective of Robert Sobel?

"Yeah, you're right. Anyway, I'd say the food was up to snuff," Rosa said, and belched lightly. "Do you want to come over and check out the house today?"

"Is Darren there?"

"I don't know," she said, looking at her watch. "Jesus, it's past three. I should go."

"Maybe I should get checked in and then drive over later."

"Sure. We'll do a late, light dinner."

"What about Margaret Clements and that business?"

"*Mañana*, honey, *mañana*. What's the rush?"

When Lucy asked her waitress for the check, she was informed that Mr. Sobel had picked it up. She looked around, and spotted him hovering over by the waiters' stand. She caught his eye and nodded thanks. He put his hands together in front of his chest, Hindu style, and bowed slightly. *Namaste*. Then he gave her that smile again.

Rosa gave Lucy directions to her house and left. Feeling flush, Lucy put a twenty on the table for the waitress. A little dazed from the alcohol and caffeine, she hauled her camera bag over to the registration desk and checked in.

The two-room suite was ruggedly plush: western-style, yes, but not so you'd suffer from lack of luxury. Under beamed ceilings O'Keeffe prints adorned the walls, Indian baskets lined the shelves, and sandy colors dominated, with Navajo rugs and patterned upholstery adding brightness to the unmatched pair of Mission-style sofas. Between them, on a rough-hewn wooden coffee table, a huge fruit basket sat next to a bottle of Dom Perignon icing in a silver bucket. Jesus! Robert Sobel was giving her the treatment.

She left the DP unopened and wandered into the next room, dominated by a canopied king-sized bed. A beehive-shaped kiva fireplace curved out of the wall opposite the foot of the bed. She passed through to the bathroom, where she admired the white marble spa tub while having a pee, then took a look in the mirror to see what Robert Sobel was interested in. Why did she care what he thought? she asked, staring at herself. Not bad for thirty-three, honey. The wrinkles are minimal in spite of all that sun, the eyes are true blue, the hair is naturally blond, and you've finally transcended cute and become, well, not knock-your-socks-off beautiful, but good looking anyway.

A tentative knock on the door popped her out of her reverie, and she let the bellhop in. His facial structure and long, braided hair signified Native American and the name on his shirt was Victor. He delivered her four bags—two holding personal items and two holding photo equipment—showed her the air and TV controls, opened the curtains, gracefully took her five bucks and thanks, then left. Lucy locked the door and went back into the bathroom to run a bubble bath with some of the locally manufactured, organic, detergent-free, herbal-essence, cell-restoring soap she found on the counter. She turned on the water, stripped, and faced her stomach in the mirror. She was guilty of daytime drinking, pasta and dessert eating, and non-exercising. For a moment she considered doing a hundred sit-ups as penance, but then the phone rang.

There was an extension on the wall by the toilet. It had to be Rosa, or Robert Sobel, she thought, picking it up. "Hello?"

"Hello, Lucy Ripken?" Neither Rosa nor Robert. The smoky croak of Madeleine Rooney. Damn!

"Yes?"

"This is Madeleine. Madeleine Rooney."

"Hi. How did you find me?"

"From Darren Davidson. I was trying to reach you at his house. Ms. Luxemburg said you'd decided to stay at the hotel."

"That's right." She waited. "What can I do for you?"

She wasted no time. "Darren tells me you are planning to write some sort of article on my—on the art he arranged to have sent up here."

"That's what I'm here for, Ms. Rooney."

"Well, you can't do that."

"Can't do that? What are you talking about?"

"You can't write about these pieces. I won't give you permission. It is simply out of the question."

"Ms. Rooney, it may surprise you to find this out, but I don't need your permission to write an article about Pre-colombian art," Lucy said, thinking, thank God I got that check and cashed it.

"About my pieces you do. About my gallery you do. Particularly if you start spreading lies and slander about the authenticity of the pieces I'm selling."

"Look, that's part of why I'm here. To find out about those pieces, and whether they're real. You know as well as I do that Quentin Washington wouldn't make up a story. There's nothing in it for him."

"I don't know what he's up to, but Herman Forte has vouched for the pieces, and his word is good enough for me."

"That's the starting point of my research. There are two expert opinions, and they're opposed. Don't you think we ought to try to get to the bottom of—"

"I think you should butt out, Lucy Ripken. I think you should do so right now. Otherwise you'll be hearing from my lawyer."

"Please, Madeleine. I can't believe you're threatening me with litigation."

"His name is Jacob Davidson, Lucy. Does the name ring a bell?"

"No."

"Well, he's Darren's father. So enjoy your stay with your friend Rosa, Miss Ripken." She hung up.

Lucy slammed the phone down. "Damn!" she said, then went over and turned off the tub, which was nearly over-flowing with a mountain of bubbles.

She stood straight and still, and began deep breathing to ease off the anger. Her fists unclenched, her breath slowed, and after a moment, she calmly climbed in the tub. She found the button for the jets, punched them on, and stretched out in the warm, churning water to contemplate the ceiling and the shifting scenario.

Lucy soaked for an hour, then rinsed in the oversized black and white checker-tiled shower, dried off, and went into the bedroom. She picked up the phone and called Rosa's house. A man answered after a single ring. "Hello?"

"Hello. Darren? Hi, this is Lucy. Lucy Ripken."

"Lucy! Hi, God I've heard so much about you I feel like we're already friends. How are you? I hear you fell into a freebie at the Anasazi Lodge. Sounds cool, but I can tell you Rosa's really disappointed, and so am I, that you're not going to be staying with us."

"Hey, I'll be there in a couple days." God, he sounded so nice! She had been readying herself for combat of a sort upon hearing his voice.

"Well, that's good. I tell ya, I'd take the hotel too if I was in your shoes. Did Rosa tell you anything about our house?"

"No, not really."

"Well, I thought it was fine till she got here, but she's been agitating to make some extensive changes, shall we say. The girl seems to think I lack taste in interior design."

He laughed. "I don't know where she got that idea, things are getting better, but it's a little Spartan around here, and I know you write about this stuff so I wanted to warn you."

"I write about it but I don't care about it, not on a personal level. Nobody I know can afford real interior design anyway. It's a racket for rich people."

"Well, you can count us—me—out of that category, Lucy. I was verging on crashing the upper middle class, but this move to Santa Fe has got me downwardly mobile, know what I mean?"

"Rosa said you were trying to write. That's definitely a good way to get poor fast."

"Yeah, I'm like a hundred and fifty pages into a novel. Doing a little lawyering on the side, but I don't have a license here so it's tricky. Teaching golf to make a few bucks. But we can catch up on all this later. When're you coming for dinner?"

"Actually that's why I called," Lucy said. The message light on her phone began blinking. "I'm so beat after flying out, and the huge lunch Rosa and I had, I think I'd rather just stay here and eat a room service salad."

"Oh, shoot. Rosa's going to be bummed."

"I know, and tell her I'm sorry. I'm just out of it. I'll come out in the morning."

"And we'll look into the Clements thing. By the way, Lucy, just so we don't have a misunderstanding: I'm sorry I gave you away to Madeleine Rooney. She has a way of getting things out of me. I've known her all my life and I still think of her as—like I'm the kid, and she's one of the adults. And I have to mind her. Anyways, I don't know exactly what the status of the whole deal is with those objects, but believe me, I have no intention of getting in your way, or letting Madeleine push you or anyone else around. And I'll do what I can to keep my father out of it, too. So don't worry. Okay?"

"Uh, yeah." What a relief! Lucy felt her anxiety slipping away. "Hey, Darren, thanks a lot for that."

"No problem. We'll pay a call on Maggie Clements tomorrow, and see what she's got to say. Hey, I think I hear Rosa, home from the store. You want to talk to her?"

"Nah, that's okay. Tell her I love her and I'll see her in the morning. Should I come there or you want to pick me up here?"

"Well, Clements lives up above Tesuque. It's out of the way, but why don't you come here. It'll give you a chance to see the house, and then I'll drive us all over there."

"See you tomorrow. Nine-ish okay?"

"We're up at dawn everyday. Rosa and her horse."

"Oh yeah! Right. Well, good night Darren. Sorry about dinner. Nice talking to you. Oh, Darren, just one thing more, about the artifacts."

"Yeah?"

"Do you know what financial arrangements have been made?"

"What do you mean?"

"Has Madeleine Rooney paid Margaret Clements for the stuff?"

He hesitated briefly. "You know, I really have no idea. I'm just not that involved. I mean, I put them together, but—why're you asking?"

"Part of the story, that's all."

"Right. *Hasta mañana.*"

"Good night."

Lucy put the phone down and began rubbing her hair dry with the towel. Darren Davidson was all right. He sounded straightforward, honest, and self-deprecating. Perfect for Rosita, that lucky girl! Good for her. One less thing to worry about in her quest to save the world for her friends, and her friends from the world.

She picked up the phone and called the front desk. "Hi, this is Lucy Ripken in the Laredo Suite. Did someone call for me a minute ago?"

"Just a moment. Yes, it was Mr. Sobel. He asked if you'd ring the bar and find him. Shall I put you through?"

"Sure." She waited.

"Hi, Lucy?"

"Mr. Sobel?"

"Please, call me Bob. Did you get checked in okay?"

"Yes. Hey, the room's great. And thanks for the champagne."

"I hope you enjoyed it."

"Honestly, after two margaritas with lunch, I didn't even open it. I took a bath, and now I'm—"

"Drink it tomorrow. Meanwhile, are you busy tonight? I thought we might have dinner together." He waited, she thought, "No way," but then he went on. "I have a little project I'm working on that I'd like to discuss with you."

The sly dog. She would have turned him down had he not thrown in that last line, which sounded like it might mean work. "I'm not too hungry, but I could do a salad, maybe."

"Great. Say around seven?"

"Eight would be better. I'm still working on lunch."

"Fine. See you then. Here in the bar for a drink first, okay?"

"Sure, Bob." She put the phone down, found the remote control, lay back on the bed, and turned on the TV for a fix of bad news.

3

Art, Artifacts, Dead Men

Lucy woke to the absence of sound: This was not New York. She lay in a fragrant bed, on linen sheets. Sunlight filled the silence with gold. Red digits read 7:17 a.m. Rosa galloped through the desert out there, horse hooves pounding. The thought made Lucy's head ache. She was hungover. Relentlessly, images from a lost evening pounded into view, counterpoint to the headache throb. They'd gone too far. She'd gone *way* too far before putting a stop to it.

Stumbling to the bathroom, she drank a large glass of cold water before getting into the shower. Enveloped in the stinging massage of hot water, she reviewed her behavior, assessing the damage.

It had begun innocently enough, although in all honesty she had gone to meet Robert Sobel with conflicted feelings up front. She didn't dislike the man, even felt a certain attraction to him. But the real reason she had agreed to the meet was the "project"—the possibility of work. She had done herself up in a somewhat seductive mode—a touch more makeup than usual, a low-cut black dress—without asking herself why. Had she more closely questioned her own motives, perhaps she would have dispensed with the bullshit, gone down there in jeans and a shirt, and talked business over a glass of mineral water.

Instead—Lucy sighed, and sank to the tile floor of the shower to wallow in the high pressure flood of hot water— she'd gone the floozy route, and dolled herself up to play games with the man.

They'd had cajun martinis at the bar, making small talk, and then segued—Lucy was already half-drunk at this point—with a bottle of wine into the dining room, where she and "Bob" had shared that bottle and another, and she'd eaten a grilled chicken salad which failed to sober her up.

Over dinner "Bob" had given her the project pitch, which had to do with a hotel he and some partners planned to build in Deer Valley, Utah. He needed pre-construction brochures written up extolling the virtues of the architecture and interior design of the new hotel. The brochures would be used to market the place to potential investors. With the design team from the Anasazi already signed on for this Utah sequel, it was a safe bet to assume the project would be of comparable quality.

With wine and dinner and more wine, Lucy had been entranced by Sobel's magnetic silvery eyes, his lovely olive skin, his simple yet elegant manners, and his mellifluous voice. Visions of mountaintop lodges danced before her, as did visions of large paychecks for easy assignments, and other visions, of herself and Robert Sobel riding off into the sunset on designer horses to his designer ranch in the hills above Taos, which he wanted to show her if she had time this week.

It had all been so smooth and seductive. Lucy should have known, the way she was swilling that fine white wine, that she was bamboozling herself on some important level. Huddled in the shower, her head throbbing and her stomach churning, she understood. But last night? No. It had been so easy to fall prey to the soft, attractive noise of too much money. For that is precisely the voice with which Robert Sobel spoke, in spite of his empathetic, low-keyed style and his New Age credentials. This was about the seductive power of money. Lucy liked money all right, she needed it like everybody else, but she had always resisted writing PR, advertising, marketing. It just wasn't worth it. Though her editorial work verged on it often enough, at least it was editorial work. Maybe the difference was semantic, but she had always insisted there was one.

Robert Sobel had offered her $5,000 to write a brochure, she had tentatively accepted, and then they had decided to mosey on up to her room to drink that bottle of Dom Perignon to ice the deal.

At the door she'd let him kiss her and then they'd gone in. Her telephone message light had been on. She ignored it. They sat on the sofa and popped the champagne cork and drank, and talked about the desert and the mountains and the 1970s, when Sobel had opened Red Sails, a restaurant on the wharf in Sausalito, launching his hip hospitality career. He had kissed her again and she had allowed him to reach inside her low-cut dress and fondle her breasts. Lucy let him work her dress down, and unhook her bra. The kissing went on, and his hands deliberately but gently moved lower, down her back, inside her panties, to rub her rear end.

"God, you've got a wonderful butt, Lucy," he murmured. "So strong."

"Thanks," she said. "It's a lot of work but—ooh, that feels great," she moaned, as he gently squeezed, working her dress and panties down as he kissed her neck, her shoulders, her breasts. He was an accomplished lover. He paused, freed his hands, and smiled at her as he reached for the champagne glasses.

"Why don't we move to the bedroom?" he said.

On the way, he'd gone to the bathroom, and Lucy had quickly called the front desk for messages. She'd gotten only one: from Harold Ipswich in New York. To call when she had a chance.

When Sobel came out he said, "Did you go to Pratt? I saw the gym bag in the bathroom."

"No, I got it from a pal."

"My daughter wants to go to art school, and that's one of her first choices. But I don't know about sending her to live in New York. What do you think?" As he sat down next to her, his intentions glowing in his eyes, she thought, I shouldn't be doing this. He's got a daughter which means he's got, or had, a wife. And he's also way older than he should be.

"I have friends that went there, and they liked it, but that was a few years back. It's way off in Brooklyn, so I don't know." Lucy watched him re-fill her champagne glass, and then reached for it. She had it halfway to her lips when she stopped and put it down. Struggling to pull herself out of the drunken swirl, she stiffened a bit. "What does her mother think?"

"Her mother?"

"Yeah. She has a mother, right?"

"Of course. But there's no need to talk about her right now, Lucy." He reached out for her.

"Wait, Bob. Just wait a minute, Okay? Are you married?"

"Her mother and I divorced years ago, Lucy, she's not an issue here at all."

"You didn't answer the question, Bob."

He gave her a look, then crossed his arms on his chest and finally said, "Yes. I'm married. But my wife—my second wife—and I have an understanding. She's in Provence right now."

"Look, Bob," Lucy said, hauling herself to her feet, willing herself sober. "I like you, I really do. I'm sorry that I led you to believe that—this—is where we were going to end up tonight." She walked to the door and opened it. "I know it's my fault too. I should have worn a suit and stopped drinking before I started. I'm sorry. And I guess at some point we should talk again about your Utah project. But you have to go. Right now."

He gazed up at her from beneath his silver eyebrows, the amorous intent abruptly drained out of him as he realized the party really and truly was over. He suddenly looked very fragile, a small, late middle-aged, irritated man. Then he threw off the rejection and rose up in all his elegant glory and came to her at the door. He took both her hands and looked earnestly into her face. But now the sexuality implied in the soft firmness of his hands only felt clammy. "I'm sorry you can't accept me on my terms. But if you only knew what I've gone through with Patricia—my wife—you'd understand."

"I don't think I'm the person you want to talk to about this, Robert," Lucy said. "I'm sorry, but I have a long day tomorrow. Thanks for dinner, the champagne, the room, the whole damn thing, but I need some sleep." She pulled her hands loose and held the door. "Good night."

Looking at once angry and forlorn, he said, "Good night, Lucy," and walked away.

But the morning after, things are always more complicated. What about Harry? And should she accept so much money for a job that she would not have been interested in at all if she wasn't persuaded as she was the night before? She needed to get back to the business she was in town to do—finding out what was going on with the Precolombian art. She would just have to put off Robert and his PR project for the foreseeable future.

Lucy dressed in slim-cut black jeans, a black T-shirt, and a blue jean jacket that had been a gift from Harold Ipswich. Quetzalcoatl, the feathered serpent of Mexican mythology, was stitched on the back in emerald green. She wore her army-green desert boots from her favorite hipster bootery on Eighth Street. She packed her purse with dark sunglasses, digital camera, extra batteries, a back-up memory chip, sunscreen, and miscellaneous junk, and headed out. She'd debated having room service breakfast to avoid the chance of a meeting with Robert Sobel, but decided that was cowardly. Instead, she went downstairs and ordered coffee, then sat on a leather sofa in the lobby, which was all morning light and Mexican tile and cacti in clay pots beneath a classic viga and latilla ceiling. She put on her sunglasses and drank her coffee, waiting for the bellhop to fetch her car.

It took ten minutes to reach Darren and Rosa's place among a dusty little strip of nondescript adobe-colored stucco houses. This was not one of Santa Fe's designer neighborhoods. A sprinkling of modulars, tumble-down trailers, and vacant lots enlivened the working class look. Several dogs lay in the dust at the side of the street, and hardly glanced up as Lucy drove past, looking for number twenty-nine. What gave away the gentrification of this particular piece of low-end Santa Fe were the cars parked in the dusty driveways outside several of the ranchitos: Range Rovers, BMWs, and Volvo station wagons. The houses that sold for $15,000 in the 1960s now sold for $250,000 plus, and spiritual seekers and trust fund refugees from both coasts had snatched them up.

Lucy spotted Rosa's blue Volvo station wagon parked in a driveway behind an old BMW with California plates, and stopped in front, where a faded white fence corralled about nine square yards of dust and a single worn piñon tree. As she approached the house she heard dogs barking inside, and Rosa, in a T-shirt, dusty jeans, and big black riding boots, opened the door before Lucy had a chance to knock. "Luce!" she said, and they hugged. "How are you? You look a little zoned out. What, this clean air bothering you?"

"Nah, I got wrecked last night," she said, as they walked into the house. "Details at five. I see you've already done your miles," she added, checking out Rosa's threads. "Sigmund," she cried, as Rosa's brown-and-white spotted mutt scooted over and jumped up on her. "Siggy, you little desert rat! I can't believe it, this dog has lost ten pounds!"

"That's 'cause he's gotta keep up with Max, my over-grown idiot cur," said Darren, coming forward to greet her. "Hi, Lucy, I'm Darren. How ya doin'?"

"Hi." Lucy shook his hand, took him in. He was just over six feet tall, wore his dark-brown hair combed back in a modified fifties kind of 'do, had brown eyes, a tan, and a slim build going thick around the middle. He wore black gym shorts, tennies without socks, and a dirty green T-shirt. He hadn't shaved in a couple of days. Though his head hair was all brown, the grizzle was gray-tinged. "Nice to meet you at last."

"Yeah, it's about time," said Rosa. "Cool out, Sig, you idiot animule," she said, as Sigmund jumped up at Lucy.

"Hey, it's all right, he misses me is all," said Lucy. "Hey Siggie, what's up? What's up, pup?" she said, roughing him up. "You smell the big city, pupster?"

"You want some breakfast, Lucy?" Darren said. "I've got an omelet on the stove."

"He cooks, too?" Lucy said, and laughed. "Such a deal! Does he do laundry?"

"Once in a while," Rosa said. "As you can tell from his shirt, it's often a very long while."

"Hey, I've been gardening, give me a break," Darren said. They wandered into the kitchen. The house was neatly furnished with old sofas, unmatched chairs, tacked-up posters, and worn-out rugs. Still a bachelor classic though Rosa had been there nearly six months. But the kitchen had a nice sunny eat-in area with a fifties' Formica-topped table, and one of Rosa's new paintings on the wall over it.

"Let's eat and then I'll show you around the place," Rosa said. "As you can see, it's no Anasazi Lodge."

"Where's all your fancy stuff from New York, Rose?" Lucy asked.

"In storage. We were planning to paint, and I figured I might as well wait. Now we're talking about getting a different place, and—hey, I don't know, my stuff's too good for the neighborhood." She grinned as Darren scowled. "Just kidding, love," she added, then went over and kissed him.

"That one of your new ones?" Lucy said, gazing at the painting of clouds over water, oil paint directly applied to a faded three-foot strip of an old one-by-twelve board that appeared to have been peeled off the side of a nineteenth-century building. "It's gorgeous."

"Um, yeah, thanks," Rosa said. "I've made a bunch of these, and I think I'm going to be able to sell them. There's a gallery on the Plaza that seems interested, and—"

"Sit down, sit down," said Darren, and pulled out a chair for Lucy. "Beat it, you dogs," he said, chasing them out the back door. "You want some coffee?"

"Sounds great." He poured her a cup, brought the food over, and they sat down to eat.

"So what's the plan?" Darren asked as they were finishing. "You want to cruise around town a little, take the tour?"

Rosa jumped in. "I thought we'd go over to my studio first."

"I've really got to talk to Margaret Clements," Lucy said, "and get to work. You didn't happen to call and tell her I was here, did you?"

"No," said Darren. "We thought it might be best if you broke the news yourself. But I'll give her a buzz and see if we can go up for a visit."

"Do you think Madeleine Rooney might have called her by now?"

"No. Maddie—Madeleine—was depending on me to handle things with Margaret."

"Does that mean she'll blame you for buying forgeries?"

"I don't know. I arranged the deal with Margaret, she had documentation, and I sent everything on by courier to Madeleine. We'll see what she has to say about it."

Rosa jumped up. "Let's go outside. I want to show you the garden."

An hour later they had seen the garden, with its wan little rows of vegetable seedlings baking in the sun, and they had driven across town and seen the studio, a one-story cinderblock bunker Rosa shared with two local talents. Paola made tapestries out of pebbles and beads and feathers, and Wanda made ceramic unicorns, dolphins, whales, and other mythical or politically correct animals, painted them with rainbows and mandalas, and sold them as fast as she could crank them out through several galleries in town.

"They're not quite New York–level artists, are they?" Rosa asked as the three of them headed out of town in Darren's BMW on the highway north toward Tesuque.

"No, not quite, Rosey," said Lucy from the backseat.

"So what is it that makes New York artists different?" said Darren, a little testily. "I think Paola's things are really nice."

"Exactly," said Rosa. "Nice. Don't tell me you think my work is 'really nice,' bub, or I'll—"

"Hey, hey, Rosa," said Lucy. "Your work is full of dialectical information about surface and reflection, and exhibits a post-Modern sense of the ironic implications of subtextual materialism. Right, Darren?"

"Is that how they talk about art in New York?" he asked.

"Nobody I know does," said Rosa. "But then, I didn't exactly conquer the art world back there, did I?" She sighed. "I suppose if I had I wouldn't have come here."

"Hey, then you wouldn't have met this guy," said Lucy. "And then what?"

"Yeah," said Darren. "Then what?"

"I don't know," said Rosa pensively. Lucy put her hand on Rosa's shoulder as they looked out the window at the rolling, piñon-covered hills. "Where does this Margaret Clements live, anyway, Darren, in a cave somewhere?"

"Hey, that's not far from the truth. She owns a mountain up here a ways, and half the house is buried underneath it." He slowed down, then turned right onto a smaller paved road leading down into the village of Tesuque—a general store and restaurant, a scattering of houses—and a moment later turned up into the hills. "It's pretty amazing, actually. Solar heated, and filled with art from all over the world. Plus she's got, like, a camel, two llamas, and a couple of ostriches."

"She collects art?" Lucy asked.

"Yeah. In a big way," Darren said. "Why?"

"Just wondered," Lucy said. Wondered why such a woman would need Darren to hook her up with Madeleine Rooney. Wouldn't she already have dealers in Santa Fe and New York if she was a serious collector?

"She's from Texas oil money," Darren said. "A trust fund babe who found her niche out in the middle of nowhere, which happens to be right about here," he went on, whipping a left turn onto an unmarked dirt road. "Now's when I wish we had a Range Rover instead of this wreck," he said to Rosa as they bounced through a pothole. "The suspension on this Beamer is history."

"Well, I may be a 'trust fund babe,' as you call it, but I'm not going to go buy you a fifty-thousand-dollar offroad toy, Darren," Rosa snapped as they crashed along on the rocky road.

"Jesus, Rosa, I didn't mean to—damn," he said, gripping the wheel. "This is a bumpy motherfucker."

"Hey, Rose, I think you took that all wrong," Lucy said from the backseat.

"Really, love, I wasn't even thinking about you when I said that. I promise." He took a hand off the wheel and reached for her. She slid over and leaned against her door, hugging herself, looking out.

"Well, maybe you should have been, *señor*. Ah, forget it. I'm sorry, I was out of line." She didn't sound at all apologetic. "Seeing Luce makes me miss New York is all. Hey, stop here a minute, Darren, I want to take a picture of Lucy and the view."

He pulled over and turned off the motor and they got out of the car. High overhead a hawk cried out, there was an echo, and then silence fell.

They had climbed above Santa Fe, now hidden by hills to the south. Above them the mountains loomed closer. A ragged cloud, softly contrasting with the depthless blue of the sky, streamed like a banner hooked on the highest peak. The piñon forests were interrupted by rocky outcroppings in beiges and sandstone reds. Higher up, the forests gave way to meadows glinting with wildflowers. The air was noticeably cooler and felt thinner. "Damn," Lucy said, gazing out into the vast distances. Her voice sounded tiny in the immensity of space. "It is something, isn't it? Makes Central Park look like somebody's backyard."

They took a few pictures, Rosa's mood improving as Lucy mugged for the camera, positioning her arms in modern dance poses meant to interpret the myriad forms of cacti, and then they continued their drive up the hill. They came over a rise abruptly, and startled a pair of odd-looking creatures gnawing on a tree at the side of the road. "Look at the llamas!" Rosa said.

"The house is just up here past those rocks," Darren said. "There are a couple of big noisy dogs, too, but they just bark a lot so don't worry."

They rounded the rocky outcropping, and the house came into view. Long and blockily graceful in the adobe pueblo style, the house's two stories appeared to hug the ground. A reddish sandstone mountain rose up behind, and the lines of the house clearly had been sculpted to echo the shape of the mountain. The architecture was classic pueblo, with a few differences: huge picture windows replaced the tiny square windows of the traditional pueblo; the basic building material was painted stucco, not adobe; and one wing of the building had a slanted roof covered with solar panels. An ostrich stood perfectly still, calmly gazing at them. Over to the right of the house, a camel stared over the top rail of a small corral.

Two Russian wolfhounds bounded into view, barking vociferously. "Jesus, they must weigh two hundred pounds apiece," Lucy said, as the enormous beasts dashed up to the car.

"Like I said, they're all bark," Darren said. Without hesitation he opened the door and got out. "Hey, Yash and Natash, how are ya?" he said, swatting at the dogs as they trotted up to him, panting and grinning. "How are you, big boys?" He scratched their heads, and they looked happy. "Not exactly fierce, are they?" Lucy and Rosa climbed out of the car. They headed up toward the house, escorted by the two giant dogs.

"Does she live alone?" Lucy said softly to Darren.

"I think so," he said. "Although I really don't know. Pretty far-out place, huh?"

"Too far-out, as far as I'm concerned," said Rosa. "I'd go nuts up here."

"Maybe that's the idea," said Darren. "She's a pretty eccentric lady."

The front door was set back deeply, an enormous oaken slab with wrought iron banding and a doorknob sculpted into the form of a coiled, sleeping snake. Darren rang the doorbell, they waited a minute, then he rang it again. No answer. They peered in the windows that flanked the door.

Suddenly the door swung open, and there stood Margaret Clements. She was fortyish, weathered by the sun, very thin, wearing old jeans, an old blue cowboy shirt, black boots, a silver studded belt, diamonds on her ears, and a red scarf over her long, dark blond, gray-tinged hair. Her eyes were pale blue and clear, with a glow to them. A million-dollar, true blue cowgirl, top to bottom. "Darren Davidson," she said, her voice a Texas drawl. "Sorry, I was in the mountain, didn't hear the bell. Howdy, Rosa. That's it, isn't it?" The timber of her voice was surprisingly frail, belying the sinewy sturdiness of her appearance.

"Yeah. Hi," said Rosa.

"Hello, Margaret," said Darren. "This is our friend from New York, Lucy Ripken. Lucy, this is Margaret Clements. Lucy's doing an article on Precolombian art."

"Darren told you I have some wonderful pieces. So you're here. As long as you don't tell anybody my name or the whereabouts of my house, you can write whatever you want about my collection." In spite of the shaky timber that made her voice sound as if it had prematurely aged, she trained her gaze, and her words, precisely on whomever she spoke to.

"Thanks," said Lucy. "I'd love to see what you have."

"Come on in," Margaret said, leading the way. They followed her into the entry. The floor was buffed flagstone; the walls were white, hand-finished textured plaster, with sculpted niches containing colorful kachina dolls and

Pueblo Indian pottery. They followed her down a long white arched hall into an enormous living room. Shelves full of Pueblo pottery lined the walls, Navajo blankets were thrown over the leather sofas, and a huge window in a wall at one end offered a stunning, endless view encompassing desert, mountains, and sky.

"Wow," said Lucy, admiring the breathtaking vista.

"I know," said Margaret. "You can almost forget about the art, with the desert to look at. You oughta see it when a storm's comin' in sometime. Like having a piece of heaven tumbling right into your lap."

"Pretty nice," said Darren. "I must say."

"This is fantastic," Rosa said. She was examining a low-slung, black and white, geometrically patterned pot set on a shelf by itself in the corner. "Is it—"

"Anasazi? Yes. I have several, but I only bring them out one at a time. The rest are in the mountain."

"Have you had this house published?" Lucy asked. "I'm sure one of the design magazines would love to do a story."

"The last thing I want is publicity," Margaret said. "And a bunch of tourists up here admiring the view."

"I could get it done anonymously. I'm sure your designer—who is your designer?—would love to see the house on the cover of, say, *Architectural Digest*."

"Actually, I designed it myself. And no, I wouldn't like to see it on the cover of anything. I'm sorry, Ms. Ripken, but I'm just not interested."

"That's fine. Please, call me Lucy. And believe me, I don't blame you. I'm just so unused to your attitude. These days most people with places like this seem to think that having them published is the main reason for building them."

"Well, I guess if I was a professional architect and I needed more work, or my ego stroked, I might feel the same way. But this is the only house I ever plan to design."

"Well, you've done a wonderful job. Would you mind if I take a few photographs, just for my own interest?"

"Of the art? Feel free. Of the house? Absolutely out of the question. In fact, you should be careful. Natasha and Yasha are very mellow, but when you put a camera up to shoot they can get quite rude."

"I see." Lucy looked at the two enormous dogs, who lay side by side on the tile floor, heads resting on crossed paws, watching. "Take it easy, kids," Lucy said. "Maybe I'll skip the photos for now."

"Well, I was just doing some work in the mountain," Margaret said. "Do you want to join me back there?"

"In the mountain?" Rosa said.

"Follow me." They did, back down the hall, through a dining room and a library, and through double steel doors into a long cool hallway sculpted out of stone. "This is where the gallery is. In the mountain. Where I keep most of the collection. The air and light are great out there. That's why I love New Mexico, but it's hard on old things. So I created this space for my collection—the lights are all UV-free." They had entered a vault-like chamber with a network of lightweight steel beams overhead supporting a sophisticated track lighting system. The floor and walls were stone. The room was occupied by display cases. There were at least a dozen, set out in neat rows on both sides of a central aisle. Each one was filled with figurines, pots, vessels, and statues. The glass cases, framed in black-finished steel, contained built-in lighting that enhanced the illumination from the overhead tracks.

"This is incredible," Rosa said, as they wandered around the vault. "You've got stuff from—"

"All over the world," Margaret said. "African, Asian, European, Mesoamerican." They stopped at a case. "This case is all Greek. I've dedicated my life to this collection. The best work I have is over here," she said, as they followed her to another case. "The Precolombians. That's where I began. When I was a kid my mother used to take us down from the ranch to the Yucatán in the winter, where we had a beach house. I bought one of these in a street market in Merida for about ten dollars." The three glass shelves housed pots, figurines, pendants, bowls, and other objects, in a variety of materials and styles. There were several similar to those Lucy had seen recently in New York. "It seemed like a lot of money at the time, but I had to have it. I just love them so much. Such power, and yet such delicacy."

"But it must have been a real bargain, even then, wasn't it?" Lucy said. "These things are practically priceless."

"It was definitely a find, because there's always been a market for this stuff. It would cost a lot more now, I'll tell you that."

"Margaret, if you don't mind my asking," Lucy said after a moment. "You seem to care so much about these objects. Why did you decide to send the Mayan pieces up to New York to sell?"

"Lucy, that's none of your business," Darren interjected.

"No, it's all right, Darren, I don't mind her asking. Actually, it's very simple. By selling the half-dozen I sent up, I make back the money I spent, so it pays for the two pieces I get to keep."

"Which are?"

"Which are what?"

"The pieces you kept. Are they here on display?"

"No, I've got another display case on order, and I'm waiting for it to be delivered. They make them in Phoenix and it takes a while with installing the special lights and all. The pieces are still in storage down in town."

"Have you had a good look at them, Margaret?"

"The new ones? Not since I bought them. Why?"

Lucy paused, glanced at Darren, and answered: "Well, it's time somebody told you. I went to the Desert Gallery the day they arrived. The other pieces you sent. I was going to photograph them for Madeleine Rooney for a catalogue. I had some friends come by to help me figure out how to shoot them, Beth and Quentin Washington, and they know their stuff—"

"Yes, I've heard of them," Margaret said.

"Well, anyways, Quentin took a look at one of the Jaina Island shell carvings, and discovered it was a fake. Then he checked the others. He's sure they're all fakes."

"Fakes? What? That's impossible."

"I'm sorry, Margaret, but—"

"Now hold on, Lucy," said Darren. "Madeleine Rooney had another expert look them over, and he wasn't so sure."

"That's true," Lucy said, "But Quentin convinced me. This other guy—his name's Forte."

"Herman Forte?" Margaret said. "I know him."

"He's not so sure they're forgeries," said Darren.

"Well, I'm sure they're not. I had them appraised and authenticated. There's no way."

"Herman Forte didn't tell Madeleine Rooney the truth because she didn't want to hear it. Darren, don't insult Margaret by doing the same thing here," Lucy said.

"Hey, wait a minute, Lucy. The issue of authenticity is not yet resolved," said Darren. "It's not like Forte is some kind of phony."

"Get serious, man. Have you met him?" Lucy said.

"Dr. Forte? No," Darren said.

"Well, take my word for it. He's not a phony, but if Madeleine Rooney told him the sky was green, he'd eventually agree, and probably find several experts to back him up."

Margaret laughed. "The hell with your experts in New York. I know one thing we can do," Margaret said. "I've got my pieces in a safety deposit box downtown. We'll just have to have another look at them. Get Calvin to come in to town and we'll check them out."

"Calvin?" Lucy asked.

"Calvin Hobart. He's the one that authenticated this stuff. He's an archaeologist, an anthropologist, and a serious collector himself. Lives up past Pojoaque toward Los Alamos. Plus his roommate—a full-blooded Mescalero Apache name of Hamilton Walking Wind—is the appraiser of the pieces. They both have impeccable reputations, I can tell you that. I'll call and ask them to hook up with us at the bank. Meanwhile, let's go back to the house. You folks can have some juice while I call."

She took them out of the mountain, locking up the steel doors, and back through the library. Then they turned left off the dining room and found the kitchen, which was huge, bright with sunshine, and homey, dominated by a big rough rectangular table under a chandelier made from an old wagon wheel. In the center of the table sat a large old wooden salad bowl filled with—Lucy could hardly believe her eyes!—peyote buttons, sitting right there, along with the bunches of herbs on the wall, and the basket of fruit on the counter, and all the tasteful accessories. Margaret brought out a bottle of organic apple juice and glasses, then picked up a phone and called while they sat drinking juice. Darren and Rosa appeared not to notice the buttons. After a minute Margaret put the phone down. "He's not answering. Probably out running. They're always out running. He and Walking Wind are jogging fools. Well, let's get down into town, I'll call again from the bank. As you can imagine I'm sort of anxious to have another look at my new babies."

"You want to ride with us? I can drive you back up later," said Darren.

"Nah, I'll get out my truck. Lucy, why don't you ride with me so that we can talk about this situation a little more, okay?"

"Sure." And so Lucy found herself driving down the mountain with Margaret Clements in a pickup truck, the two pony-sized dogs in the back, one on each side, heads out, grinning in the jetstream.

"I'm sorry you didn't get a chance to shoot pictures of the art, Lucy," Margaret said as they bounced down the dirt road. "You'll have to come up again."

"I was hoping you'd say that. But first you've got to resolve this problem with the fakes."

"If they are."

"Right." Why argue? She liked this woman. "If you don't mind my asking, Margaret, who's your source for the pieces?"

"Oh, that's confidential, Lucy. Everybody's got their own connections, you know. You're not gonna find any collectors willing to talk about that. See, since the UNESCO laws passed a few years back it's against the law to bring this stuff over the border. You can't get legitimate documentation on smuggled goods. But I've been buying from the same people for a while, and they've never sold me fakes. I will tell you that."

"The issue of fakes aside, doesn't it bother you to be involved in the market for illegal goods? National treasures of Mexico and all that?"

"Well, I don't buy in the black market unless something really hot comes up. Besides, if I thought the pieces would end up in one of the museums down there it would bother me. But if they're going to end up in private collections anyway, which is what happens to almost everything that gets dug up these days, it might as well be up here instead of down there, way I see it."

"So why not be a hero and buy the stuff and simply give it back to the museum down there? Repatriate it to the Mexican government?"

"I tried that once. Found myself seriously harassed by people on both sides of the border, who put the squeeze on me to discover my sources. Plus I returned four pieces and only two ended up in the museum. The other two I'm told were put in storage, but no one's seen them since."

"So the system is so hopelessly fucked up that all you can do is play along, contribute to the mess."

Margaret looked at her. "Yeah, I guess that's one way of seeing it. On the other hand, I have to admit I love owning them. I love having them. I don't have any kids—I gave up on marriage after my third—so between my animals and my art, well, they're my babies. I look at them, I spend hours in the mountain every day, just looking at them. I love knowing they're mine."

"Yeah, I guess I can understand that," Lucy said, although she really couldn't. Oh, she could understand the aesthetic attraction of the pieces, all right. What she couldn't understand, or chose not to, was the possessiveness, the hunger for having, that underpinned Margaret's attitude. The operative word was "mine."

"So tell me, Margaret. You've obviously been involved with this stuff for a while. Why did you decide to work with Darren Davidson and Madeleine Rooney? Didn't you know dealers in New York before?"

"Sure. But Darren told me Rooney could turn them around quickly, at higher prices, with a smaller commission. She's got good connections. It was strictly business."

They made their way into town, and soon arrived at the Santa Fe National Bank, which happened to be directly across the street from the Anasazi Mountain Lodge. As they pulled into the parking lot, Lucy saw a slightly unnerving sight out of the corner of her eye: Robert Sobel and Darren Davidson chatting amiably just inside the open entrance to the hotel lobby. "Well, here we are," Margaret said, pulling into the lot next to the BMW, in which Rosa still sat. "I assume you all want to come in and have a look with me?"

"Yes, I sure do. But I need to make a phone call first. I'll catch up to you. Hey, Rosa," she added, as Rosa got out of the car. "Where's the husband material?"

"Surprise, surprise," she said. "Darren knows your pal Robert Sobel. He ran into him in the street, and they're over there chatting." She nodded in the direction of the hotel. Lucy glanced at the two men.

"Small town, eh?" she said. "I've seen enough of that dude for now. Hey, listen, I need to make a call," she added. "I'll catch up to you in the bank."

Lucy tried her cell, couldn't get through, then found a pay phone on the corner and called the museum in New York. It was noon in Santa Fe, two p.m. in New York, and Quentin had promised to be near a phone. He answered on one ring. "Museum, hello."

"Hi, it's me, I'm in Santa Fe."

"Hey, how is it?"

"Fine. Actually, the whole damn town is so tasteful it hurts. But we're at the bank, where Margaret Clements has the other pieces in a safety deposit box."

"Other pieces?"

"From the same lot. Same source as the fakes. Seeing them should help get things sorted out. I'll be looking for . . . ?"

"I don't know if you'll be able to. Well, what the hell, give it a try. Steel tool marks, like we discussed, look different from jade saw marks. You'll need a magnifying glass. Also, the iconography might look incongruous or—I don't know, there's really no way to do it without experience, Luce."

"Well, I tend to trust my instincts on things like this."

"Don't be arrogant, Lucy. It takes years to learn this stuff."

"All right, all right. Sorry. I'll play it by ear, okay?"

"Just don't make any bad calls. The stakes are too high. And it's not your job."

"Right. Also, I wanted to ask you, have you ever heard of a guy named Calvin Hobart?"

"Calvin Hobart." He mulled over the name, then came into focus. "Yeah, yeah, I remember him from school in Austin. He was a grad student, assistant professor. Went on to make a decent name for himself teaching in Tucson. He knows his stuff, that's for sure. Has a solid reputation. What's up?"

"Well, he lives here now. He appears to be the man responsible for the letters of authentication, such as they may be."

"Really. Well, damn, I'd sure like to see these rumored letters. Listen, I don't know if he'll remember me, but say hey to him, remind him of Austin '75 and mention my name. And then ask him what the hell he's doing putting his imprimatur on bogus goods, the dumb fuck."

"Can I quote you on that?"

"Sure, why not, that's exactly what he's being if he thinks that junk is real. Where did she get it, anyway? Did she tell you that?"

"No way. Trade secret, she says."

"I'm not surprised. Probably got a fake factory just humming along somewhere down there. Hey, by the way, was her collection as awesome as I've heard?"

"Pretty impressive. You oughta see the pad. And listen, I have to say, if there's any kind of scam going on here, I don't think she's part of it. She's too—I don't know—spacey, and yet real, at the same time, to be hustling fakes."

"That's a pretty ambiguous rap, Lucy."

"Well, picture this: She's designed her own enormous pueblo-modern pad up on her private mountain, she's got millions of dollars' worth of art stashed in a custom-designed cave behind the house, and guess what's sitting right in the middle of her kitchen table?"

"I don't know, a voodoo doll?"

"A giant wooden salad bowl, filled with peyote buttons!"

"Jesus Christ! You're kidding me!"

"No. There they were, like so many ugly little shriveled-up apples. I couldn't ever mistake the sight, not after the one and only time I tried some. Which happened here, like, fifteen years ago. You ever chew any of those nasty critters?"

"Sure. Every week at first when I was going to school down there in Austin. We had a Navajo pal and he got them for nothing. But my stomach couldn't take it. So I switched to acid. Much easier to digest."

"Yeah, but not organic, man."

"When you're looking to get cosmic, organic doesn't matter. Not puking for six hours straight does. Am I right?"

"It was righteous puking, though, wasn't it? Could hear echoes of eternity in those retches, as I remember it. Well listen, I guess I should sign off, I'm pretty busy."

"Just keep your eyes open, honey. And your mitts out of the peyote jar."

"No way I want to walk that walk again. Hey, love to Beth. Later."

"Okay, Luce. Take care."

A bank official guided her to a private room in the back, where she found Rosa, Darren, and Margaret seated at a conference table. There were two objects on the table, distinctly different from any she'd seen before. One was a cylindrical ceramic vessel, completely plated all around with a mosaic of small squares of jade, seamlessly joined. The vessel was covered by a lid with a sculpted three-dimensional jade head on top, surrounded by richly detailed illustrations carved into the sloping surface of the lid. The second piece was a life-size jade portrait mask, with some indentations where precious stones had probably been removed. Lucy could see that these two pieces, whether real or fake, were the stars of the show. "So here they are," said Margaret. "Still look as real as rain to me."

"I don't know what makes for fakes in this field," said Darren, "But they look good to me."

"May I?" Lucy asked Margaret as she sat down and picked one up.

"Sure, just be careful," Margaret answered.

"Right." Lucy whipped out her magnifying glass and delicately turned the mask around, upside down, and sideways, checking the surface carefully for the steel cut marks Quentin had described as indications of fakery. She couldn't find any. She wondered if she didn't know enough. She knew she didn't know enough. She knew she couldn't tell the difference between Iranian Jade and Mexican Jade. For all she knew this could be Iranian, which would date it late twentieth century. She put it down and carefully lifted the lid off the vessel, and looked it over. Same deal. She put it down. They all looked at her. "Well, I was looking for something that would tell me these were fakes, and I can't find it, so I don't know."

"What, a 'Made in Taiwan' sticker, perhaps?" said Darren.

"Really, Lucy, what are you looking for?" Rosa added.

"Okay, okay, I'll tell you what I'm doing," she said. "Quentin Washington explained that if you looked closely enough you could tell fake jade pieces by the cut marks, the tool marks. The fakes were usually made with steel tools, and they left marks unlike the stone tools of the originals. Also sometimes they make the forgeries with jade from foreign countries, and it looks different. Everything else can be duplicated perfectly, but the tone of the jade and the tool marks give them away."

"And you don't see the right color, or any such tool marks on these?" asked Darren in a lawyerly fashion.

"No, but—"

"But what?" Darren said.

"I don't know enough about the color, or about reading the marks. Plus I don't see why forgers couldn't just start using stone tools, too," Lucy said.

"Hell, Lucy," said Margaret. "Sounds to me like you're downright disappointed these might be real."

"No, it's not that. I'm just irritated because I don't feel competent," she said. "I thought I would know exactly what I was looking for, and that I would find it. But it seems pretty nebulous now."

"Maybe that's because these aren't fakes, Lucy," said Darren.

"Let me try Calvin again," Margaret said. She picked up the phone on the table. "Hello, could you give me an outside line, please? Thanks." She paused, then punched in a number. After a moment, she put the phone down. "Still no answer. If they were out jogging, they would have come back by now. The machine's off. I don't know, seems strange, those guys never go anywhere." She looked around the table. "You folks feel like taking a ride?"

"To Hobart's?" Darren asked.

"Yeah. Maybe the phone's busted and they don't know it. Stranger things have happened."

"Sure," said Lucy.

"He and Hamilton have a gorgeous house, too, so you'll get a kick outta that," Margaret said. "You want to drive, Darren? We should take only one car and I think we'd be more comfortable in yours. We'll just put these two babies in a bag and take 'em with us. Save Calvin the trouble of coming back to town."

Margaret left the dogs in the back of her truck in the bank parking lot in the middle of town. This was not New York. They headed out. They soon passed the turnoff to Tesuque and continued north, then northwest. The road soared upward, winding through a sandstone canyon, and in the midday glare the high desert appeared desolate in spite of the piñons, the rocky buttresses, and the mountains rising in the distance. Lucy and Margaret rode in back, the two bubble-wrapped artifacts in a canvas Santa Fe National Bank moneybag on the seat between them.

A few miles out of Pojoaque they turned off the main drag onto a dirt road that curved up toward a rocky rise about a mile distant. "The house is just under the hilltop up yonder," Margaret said. "You wouldn't find it if you didn't know it was there. See, right there," she pointed toward the right side of the butte, where a rambling wood and adobe structure hugged the hillside. Sun glinted off a tin roof, flashing in their eyes. The sky was utterly empty of clouds.

As they approached the house, details came clear. There was a semi-circular gravel driveway with a Range Rover and a pickup parked to one side. The house featured deep porches under slanted red tin roofs supported by white posts and beams, and an eye-pleasing mix of peaked and flat rooflines. The forward thrust of the building, with flanks flowing back at right angles at both ends, suggested the presence of an enclosed courtyard behind the central wing.

Darren parked by the dusty green Range Rover, and the four of them got out. As the sound of the last car door slamming shut died away, they were stilled by the silence, which was not so much silence but rather an insistent, indirect whispering caused by the small soft noise of the wind in the brush, the rocky canyons, and in the eaves of the house.

They walked toward the front door, and the sound of their feet in the gravel echoed unnaturally loud in the desert air. The yard was an exquisite orchestration of desert plants and cacti, so perfectly placed as to seem accidental, naturally occurring, except that the hand of a landscape designer was given away by the presence of a few scatterings of brightly colored flowers and two small, freeform, rock-lined pools flanking the path leading to the front porch. A pair of Mission-style rocking chairs and a small leather-topped table occupied one side of the porch. Lucy thought she heard a dog whining just before Margaret knocked vigorously on the raised panel door. "They're usually out back by the pool or in the studio, so you gotta beat on this damn door or they won't hear at all," she said.

"Did you hear a dog?" Lucy asked.

"No, did you?" Darren said.

"I thought so. Not a bark, a whine."

"Didn't hear a thing," Rosa said. "Except maybe the sound of my blood flowing. Damn, it's quiet out here."

"They've got a poodle. A white standard named Claud. Mighta been him," Margaret said, and beat on the door again. "Hey, Calvin, you there? Ham, you guys home?" She tried the doorknob. It was unlocked. She pushed it open a foot. "Calvin, you home?" she said, leaning halfway into the house. "Hey, Walking Wind, you here?" There was no answer. Margaret pushed the door farther open, and they followed her in, tentatively.

They were in a large entry area, with arched doorways on both sides. Straight ahead a pair of open glass-paneled doors let onto a patio. Across the patio the blue of a swimming pool sparkled in the sun. "Where are those boys?" Margaret said. Suddenly a large white poodle bounded in through the patio doors, barking and whining. "Hey, Claud, how are you?" Margaret went on, as the poodle rushed over and leaped up, excited to see her. With his hair cut short, he looked like a regular dog, not at all frou-frou. He had large, intelligent brown eyes, and a brown nose. "Good dogster. Now where's your dad, huh? Where's Mr. Calvin?" She rubbed his ears and head. "That's the living room in there," she said, waving at a doorway. "And yes, that is an original O'Keeffe. They own three."

"Great house," said Lucy, as she and Rosa paused in the doorway and took in the living room. It had a high, beamed ceiling, a fireplace sculpted out of the wall, the O'Keeffe flower, and half a dozen other paintings on the walls. There were Navajo blankets on the leather sofas, shelves of pueblo pottery and statuary, and kilims on the pine floors. It was warm and light and airily comfortable, thoughtfully arranged and accessorized without being the least bit intimidating. Lucy liked the owners of the house before meeting them, always a good sign.

"Really charming," said Rosa. "I thought Santa Fe style was so passé back in New York, and it's total overkill down in town, but when you see it done right it looks good again."

"I'm gonna go outside and let Claud find Calvin for me. Feel free to sit down and relax a minute if you'd like," Margaret said. "These boys are very informal."

"No, we'll go, too," said Lucy. "I'd love to see the rest of the house and grounds anyways."

"Definitely," said Darren. "I'm beginning to understand why you don't like my furniture and stuff, honey," he said. "I guess I just haven't thought much about it, is all."

"No, not much, babe," Rosa said. "Maybe Calvin will give you a few lessons."

They followed Margaret and the whining white poodle out the French doors onto the patio. Claud's barking level abruptly ratcheted up in frequency and volume as he whirled around, leaping into the air. "Jesus, what's wrong, Claud?" Margaret said. "Take it easy, pup. I've never seen this dog so riled up." They came out from under the porch roof into the blinding glare of direct sun, and Lucy slipped her shades on as they walked toward the pool, Claud in a frenzy now. Nobody spoke; nobody had to, because they all knew something was very wrong, and whatever it was waited here, at the pool, drawing them forward. "Oh, Lord," Margaret said, the first to reach poolside. "Omigod." The four of them stopped, lining up along the tiled edge of the pool.

Lucy took it all in a sun-blasted revelation: the freeform pool with the feathered serpent Quetzalcoatl tiled on the bottom; and rippling over it the shadows of the two bodies that floated facedown, bloated, wearing bathing suits and roasted to a dark shade of pink by the sun, on the surface of the pool. "Oh no, oh no, oh no," said Margaret, hands to her mouth.

"Jesus Christ," said Darren. "Jesus fucking Christ. Don't touch anything. Christ. I'll call the police. Where's the phone? Margaret, where's the goddamn phone?" he shouted.

"Hey, take it easy, Darren," Lucy said. "Don't shout at her!"

"Is that Calvin?" Rosa whispered. "Are you sure it's him?"

"Who else could it be?" Margaret croaked. "And Hamilton. See the long hair? Oh, see the long black hair? Oh Lord."

"Damn, this phone's not working," Darren said. He'd found a cordless on a patio table. "Rosa, see if you can find a phone. But don't touch—don't—wait, I'll go with you, what if the killer is still—"

"I don't think anyone's here," Lucy said. "The dog wouldn't have been so whacked out. Come here, pup," she went on, calling Claud. He came over, whining more softly now, and lowered his head as he stood before her. "Poor baby. Poor, poor baby. This poor animal's been guarding them." She petted the dog, then forced herself to look at the bloated bodies. "Waiting for God knows how long. A few days, anyway." In an effort to stay calm, she unzipped her bag and pulled out her digital camera. She turned it on, pointed it at the pool, and started snapping.

"Jesus, Lucy, is that necessary right now?" Darren said.

"As a matter of fact, yes," Lucy said. "Absolutely." She knew they were all in shock, and that they would miss important things; and that the police, when they came, would probably destroy half the evidence before they even laid eyes on it.

Margaret had collapsed into a lounge chair. Lucy went over to her. "Are you all right? Can I get you a glass of water or something?"

"No, I'm fine. It's just—I've known Calvin for at least twenty years. He was the most peaceable man. He and

Hamilton were so perfect together." She burst into tears. "Who in the hell would do this? Why?"

Lucy had another look at the pool. "I don't know, Margaret. I just don't know. They have a lot of art here, and—"

"But it's not even gone, Lucy. You saw the O'Keeffe. That and the Precolombian pieces are the most valuable things they have."

"Where are those? Where did they keep them?"

"The Precolombians? There's a gallery off their bedroom. Over there." She gestured toward the house, then collapsed further into the chaise. The curtains were drawn on the French doors. Lucy walked around the pool, capturing images of the bodies, the patio, and the exterior walls of the house from several angles.

"The phone was unplugged," Darren said, as he and Rosa came back out on the patio. "The machine's been completely erased, of all incoming messages and their greeting. I called the state police. They'll be here ASAP, they're sending a chopper," he barked.

Lucy wandered into the house and through the living room, pausing to take a couple of shots. She saw nothing amiss. She passed through a doorway under a heavy wooden lintel and entered a long hallway. Windows on her right faced the patio and the pool. On her left, doors opened on a bedroom, a bathroom, another bedroom, and then an arch opened into the master bedroom and gallery.

The gallery room included an office area and a number of shelves and display cabinets full of Precolombian pieces from different eras. She went directly to the Mayan shelves. There were three pieces that she thought probably dated from the same era as those she'd seen in New York—two of the shell carvings, and a jade pendant similar in style to Margaret's mosaic vessel in the car. She snapped a slide of the pendant, up close; as she did so, something caught her eye. She looked more carefully. Were those steel tool marks? She pulled out her magnifying glass and picked the piece up to look underneath. Damn, she needed Quentin right now. She put it down quickly and picked up the pendant for a look. The same thing. A couple of fakes. Maybe.

She set the pendant down, shot some close-ups, and then backed away. As she turned to leave, Darren, standing in the doorway, said, "What's up, Lucy?"

"I don't know," she said. "Just looking."

"Hey, I'm sorry I yelled out there," he said.

"I know. It's horrible, and very upsetting. Hey, how's Margaret?"

"She's better. But how about you?"

"I'm curious," she said. "I put up the camera like this," she went on, holding it before her eyes, "And I can remove myself from the immediacy of the situation. It's a form of—"

"Protection?" he finished for her.

"Something like that," she said. She moved to the door of the bedroom. "You want to have a look around in here?" she said. "What a beautiful room."

Darren followed her into the master bedroom, an enormous room with a peaked, beam ceiling. A king-sized bed with a wrought iron frame and an antique quilt spread dominated the space. There were two O'Keeffes, one over the bed, one on the wall opposite, next to a hammered tin Mexican mirror that rested atop an antique chest of drawers. A kiva-style fireplace curved out of the corner, with a pair of leather-upholstered club chairs in front, and hand-knit rugs were spread across the wood floor. The walls were white, hand-finished plaster, and two of them had huge windows with views of the desert on one side and the pool and patio on the other.

The dog bounded into the room and leaped up on the bed. "Hey, Claud," she said. "Come here, pup." He flew off the bed, sliding on a rug, then jumped over to her. She pocketed the camera and opened her arms to the big poodle, with his raggedy white hair cut so unlike the topiary shrub cuts she'd seen on every poodle she'd ever encountered. Claud had refused to leave, though he'd been free to do so for days, with his masters dead in the pool. What would happen to him?

By the time the state police got there ten minutes later, in a cloud of dust and a roar of chopper blades, she had decided. She would take him home to New York City. She convinced Margaret, Darren, and Rosa to concur with her story—that they'd brought the dog out with them on the visit to Calvin's, that he was Rosa's from back East, and that he was missing New York so much Lucy had agreed to take him home to the city. A fine set of lies, but Claud wasn't exactly an expert witness, so the cops wouldn't mind, most likely, even if they did find out.

It took a couple of hours to go through the routine with the state police. The team was headed up by a guy named Sam Rodriguez, a tall, gaunt Chicano with a tooth-pick under a black mustache, a huge cowboy hat, and black boots that gleamed like obsidian in the sun. He didn't waste their time, they didn't waste his: He asked the basic questions and got the essential information, then told them to stick around town in case he needed them for further questioning. Soon they were on their way back in the BMW with the artifacts, still of questionable provenance, now in the trunk since Claud the dog had taken over the center of the backseat. Lucy kept a hand on his head and gently scratched him the whole way back to town. They were quiet, mulling over what had just happened. "You guys want to get a drink somewhere, maybe talk this over?" Lucy said.

"How 'bout at our house?" Rosa replied. "I don't think you can take a dog—even a poodle—into the bars around here."

"Sounds good," said Margaret. "Let me get my truck, I don't want to leave the dogs alone any longer, and I'll meet you all. Where is your place?"

"I'll ride with you," Lucy said. "I know the way. Hey, you have anything to eat up there? I haven't had a thing since the omelet, and this may sound crass, but I'm hungry."

"So am I. I'll make some bean tostadas," Rosa said.

"We'll pick up some beer. See you in a minute," said Margaret as Darren and Rosa left them in the parking lot. Claud had bounded right into the truck with Yasha and Natasha, and the three of them were engaged in a butt-sniffing round. Claud was a little intimidated by the two monsters, but they were easy on him, as if they understood how large they loomed over him. Lucy had fed him some dried food while they waited for the police, and he'd inhaled it. He had been starving, but he had not left his master.

They stopped at a mini-mart for beer. Lucy bought a can of gourmet dog food, and they headed over to Darren and Rosa's.

"God, what a day," Lucy sighed.

"Hellish, huh," Margaret said. "Those poor boys. Lord, what happened out there?"

"I don't know, but I can't help but wonder if it had anything to do with the objects."

"What, the new Precolombian stuff?"

"Yeah. It's a weird coincidence, don't you think, that the stuff in New York turns out to be forged?"

"Maybe."

"Right. Maybe. And then to have the man responsible for authenticating them die like that, in his own home."

"I guess you figured out that he and Hamilton had a— you know, they were—"

"Gay? Yeah. Doesn't seem relevant to me, Margaret."

"Well, maybe not, but—"

"But what? What are you getting at?"

"Forget it."

"By the way, Margaret, if you don't mind my asking you—you might want to think about this before that cop Rodriguez comes up to your house for the 'further questions' routine, anyway. What do you do with the bowl of peyote buttons on your kitchen table? I mean, do you—"

"Take them? Yes, as a matter of fact I do. I've been an honorary member of the Native American Church for years now. I make tea from buttons and do a voyage once a month, usually with the full moon. Drink it and—"

"Throw up?" Lucy said.

Margaret laughed. "No, I fast for a day, sleep lightly, get up at dawn, and drink my tea. I cook a gallon down to a pint with twenty-four buttons, then drink it with lemon and honey. Tell the truth, I've grown rather fond of that nasty flavor over the years. And it's a great way to stay in touch with your spirits."

The woman was totally psychedelicized. Probably explained the haunt in her voice, the glow in her eyes. "I can imagine. But put 'em away when the cops come, Margaret. They're illegal."

"Not if you're in the Native American Church."

"I think the Rehnquist court trashed your church a few years back. Just be careful. These days the cops take their drug busts very seriously. Here's their street," Lucy said. They parked behind Lucy's rental car. Claud, Yasha, and Natasha jumped out the back end of the truck and ran ahead of them to the front door. Lucy rapped on the door, which swung open, and the three of them entered. Darren, Rosa, and the two resident mutts appeared, and there was the usual frenzy of sniffing and jumping around as Max and Sigmund met Claud and the big dogs. Darren led the way into the kitchen, where he and Rosa had set up a tostada supper at high speed.

They ate, drank beer, talked a little. After the food, as they cracked a second round of beers, Lucy said, "So, just so we know what to say when Rodriguez calls our separate numbers, I was wondering, Margaret. I know you don't want to give up any names, but if they do somehow link it up with the Precolombian thing, and I think it might happen since that was Calvin's area of expertise, and everybody knows there's a lot of money in that market these days—anyways, maybe you oughta let us know at least, like, where the stuff came from?"

"The Mayan stuff all comes from the same area," she said. "Down in the Yucatán. Around Merida. Chichen Itza, Tulum, all the Yucatán Mayan sites. That's the area. It doesn't all necessarily originate there, but it seems to end up there. I guess because there are so many archaeologists and fortune hunters in the neighborhood. Plus dope runners and all kinds of Caribbean vagabonds, some with a lot of money in their pockets."

"Not far from where your family has that beach house, huh?"

"Yeah. Not too far." So they still owned it.

"You been down lately?"

"To the house? No, not in years. Why are you asking?"

"I'm just playing devil's advocate, Margaret. These are the threads the cops might try to tangle you with. Does your family still use the house?"

A slight hesitation. "No."

"What about your brother?"

She blanched. "How did you know I had a brother?"

"I didn't. A guess. Most people do, it seems. Where's he hang out?"

"Oh, he's around, I don't know. Travels a lot."

"You seen him lately?"

"Lucy, what is this, the third degree?" Darren said. "Back off, you're not a cop."

"Sorry. No, just a journalist in this case."

"No, that's all right," said Margaret. "I don't mind." She took a hit of beer. "Nathaniel's a—that's my brother, Nate—he's—oh, hell, why should I bullshit you? He's the one that brought this stuff over the border. He set the whole thing up. He's not my usual source, but when Calvin checked the pieces out and said they were authentic, I figured I had nothing to lose, keep it in the family. Nate told me he got them down there. From a local collector looking for hard cash. I mean, they were smuggled in, but they were already in a private collection." She shrugged, and took a hit off her beer bottle. "It's not like they were recent finds."

"Nate lives at the beach house?"

"Sometimes. It's kind of falling apart. Nobody's used it, except him, in years."

"Is he down there now?" Lucy asked.

"I don't know. I guess he could be. There's no telephone, last I heard, so I couldn't really tell you. I suppose we could try a telegram."

"How about we try a personal appearance?"

"What are you talking about, Lucy?" Darren interjected.

"Let's go down there," she said. "All of us. There's something serious going on with this stuff, I'm doing this story, and wouldn't it be great to go to the beach?"

"I can't go to Mexico, I've got work to do," said Darren. "Besides, that cop's not going to let you leave town."

"Hey, we didn't do anything, we don't know anything, we have nothing to hide," said Lucy. "Forget about the cop. He'll forgive us, and even if he doesn't, so what? Call it a trial honeymoon, you guys." She smiled at Rosa and Darren.

"Hell, I haven't been down in years," said Margaret. "We can stay at the house. I'm game. Rosa?"

Rosa looked at Darren, who stared fixedly at the label on his beer bottle. "I'd love to go," she said. "I haven't seen the ocean in six months."

4

Big Fun in the Yucatán

The next day Lucy left her new dog in the care of Margaret's factotum, an ageless, taciturn Native American named Jedediah Crowtooth who lived in a tidy little two-story adobe hut around the mountain from Margaret's pueblo. Lucy sneaked out of the hotel with a last-minute "Thanks, see ya later, stay in touch" note to Bob Sobel, and drove her companions to Albuquerque, where the three women boarded a commuter plane for the hop to Dallas.

Lucy made calls during the two-hour layover in Texas. Heidi was pleased that the story had developed so quickly, and was especially thrilled at the introduction of death into the narrative. She begged Lucy to email the images she'd shot at Calvin Hobart's ranch. Though she understood Heidi's morbid excitement Lucy demurred. She wanted to keep those to herself for a time. She left the memory chip holding them in Margaret Clements's safety deposit box at the bank.

Quentin gave her the lowdown on Alberto Gutierrez, who lived on the outskirts of the little town of Ticul in the Yucatán. Famed in art and anthropological circles for his brilliant re-creations of Mayan statuary and pottery, Gutierrez sold signed knock-offs in a range of Precolombian styles to the tourists. Rumor had it he dug up the occasional pre-interred high-quality forgery whenever he judged the market could bear some fresh product.

Harold, sober as a judge, declared himself ready to meet her in Mexico when he heard about the dead men in the pool and her ensuing dash for the border. When she discouraged that possibility he gave her the names of three restaurants, one in Merida, one in Cancún, and one on Isla Mujeres, along with the names of the proprietors and best bets off each menu. The last thing he said to her was "I love you." Lucy murmured the words back at him, wondering why she had to leave town to hear them.

Fifteen minutes later boarding was announced. Cancún-bound, the three women strolled onto the Mexicana Airlines jet, took over the first-class compartment, and had their flight attendant uncork a bottle of champagne. This was not exactly a vacation, but Lucy felt giddy in spite of the dead men in Santa Fe. She hadn't known them; people died every day. Maybe she could find out why they had. Meanwhile, she was traveling first class to Mexico with girlfriends, on an adventure, on assignment! What in the world could be better?

When Harold had suggested that he fly down to meet her, her initial reaction had been enthusiastic. "Great!" she'd said—and immediately regretted it.

He heard her voice fall by the end of the one-syllable word. "Right," he replied flatly. "Great." He paused. "No, I think I'll leave you to your pals." He paused again, to give her a chance to change his mind. She didn't. "So keep me posted, Luce. Be careful. And remember: I love you."

Now, back in her black-and-white traveling garb, sipping champagne in first class, facing her new friend and her old friend across a little table elegantly set with a fruit and cheese platter amidst crystal, white linen, and champagne flutes, Lucy said a silent thanks to Harold for leaving her alone. She loved the men in her life, and yearned for them when they faded away, but her real emotional touchstones had always been her girlfriends. Women knew how to talk, and more important, how to listen. Not that Harold was a bad conversationalist. He certainly paid attention, how else would he have copped such a quick read on that phone call? But lately, his emotional dialogue was too dependent on therapy and Twelve-Step training. When he wasn't drinking he tended to get self-righteous, and when he drank, he confessed. Either way it got to be a bore.

She chased him out of mind and smiled at Rosa, dressed in her usual faded jeans and T-shirt, this one white, with the short sleeves turned up. All she needed was a tattoo and a Camel in her mouth. She'd traded in the cowboy boots for a pair of black sports sandals. "You pack an extra snorkel for me, Rosita?" Lucy asked.

"Three snorkels, six fins, and number forty sunscreen. We are ready. I read where the water off this beach called Playa Garrafon is absolutely thick with tropical fish."

"And boatloads of gringos from Cancún on daytrips," said Margaret, wearing a black silk cowgirl dress with gold trim and pearl buttons. She even had a little makeup on. "Forget Garrafon. It used to be incredible, but ever since they invented Cancún it's been overrun."

"So where do we go to dive, Margaret?" Lucy said. "We have to dive somewhere."

"Maggie. Didn't I tell you to call me Maggie?" She smiled. "If it's calm I know a reef not far from the house," she said. "We can take a boat out. There's a big ol' cave full of sharks."

"Great," said Rosa. "Sharks."

"They're nice sharks," Maggie said. "Nurse sharks. Friendly as dogs. They won't bother you unless maybe you swim up and punch one upside the head."

"When's the last time you were down here, Maggie?" Lucy asked. "Has it been a while?"

Maggie hesitated. "Yes. A few years. I spent so much time on Isla when I was a kid, I kind of lost interest later on. And the house is—well, y'all see soon enough."

"What about your brother?"

"Nate? I don't see him that often, so I don't really know what he's up to, but yes, he's been parked down there on and off. He and Daddy don't get along too well."

"What's the problem?"

Maggie paused, and finished off her glass of champagne. "Don't get me wrong. Nate . . . Nathaniel's a great guy, he's an original, and he's always gonna be my one and only kid bro, but he's, well, you know, kind of a post-sixties vagabond. Had some problems in the past, and Daddy runs a mean streak. I don't get along with Daddy too well myself, but he doesn't take women seriously anywhich, so it doesn't much matter. The way he sees it, I'm just eccentric like my mama was, but Nate likes to gamble, and party, and play the saxophone. He was always the real rebel, in and out of trouble."

"What happened to your mother?" Lucy asked softly.

"Oh, I don't know," she said offhandedly, averting her eyes. "I mean—she died."

"I'm sorry," said Lucy. "I didn't mean to pry."

"That's okay. I just don't talk about it, or even think about it much these days."

"Listen, my mother's been watching my father get drunk for the last twenty-five years. I don't think about them much either," Lucy said. "Unless I have to."

"My mother and father haven't slept in the same room since 1975," said Rosa. "In fact, they inhabit separate wings in the manse." She raised her glass. "Welcome to the dysfunctional family club."

"And look at us," said Maggie. "Not doing a whole lot better, are we?"

"Hey, don't give me this dysfunctional jive," said Lucy. "That kind of talk's for *Oprah* addicts. Being independent isn't so bad."

"I guess not," said Maggie wistfully. "But sometimes it just means being alone, doesn't it?"

"I got a boyfriend," said Rosa.

"And he's smart, handsome, and a lawyer at that," said Lucy, with a lighten-up smile. "So what about this Isla Mujeres, Maggie? What's the story?"

Nathaniel the bad-boy brother intrigued Lucy. He sounded like an interesting shipwreck of a man. Thirty-three like her, never had a job, on the outs with Daddy, played the blues on the tenor saxophone, used to have a serious speedball—junk and coke—habit but kicked it, still living the wild life though Daddy'd disinherited him and he apparently had nowhere to go but here, up the road, to the decaying family digs on Isla Mujeres.

Island of the Women. The origin of the name, Maggie had said, was explained by a couple of different legends. Take your choice: One had it that Caribbean pirates had stashed their female kidnap and ransom victims there; the other said the Maya had left hundreds of statues of Ixchell, the female deity, on the isla en route south to the larger island of Cozumel, which was sacred to her.

All blue sky, white surf, and green jungle in relentless light, the go-slow ambience of the Yucatán coast of Quintana Roo greeted them as they walked off the plane and into the oven. The hot wind blew in hard off the chop-ripped sea, snapping the flags, and Lucy started thinking windsurf. Twenty knots of salt air and a warm ocean waiting. "So now what?" said Rosa, a little worn. She was not accustomed to daytime drink. None of them were.

"Rent a car, drive to Punta Sam, and take the ferry to Isla," said Maggie as they headed over toward the new terminal building. "Damn, I forgot how hot it gets here. This humidity is too much."

"Tell me again why we're here, Lucy," said Rosa, wilting fast in spite of the breeze. "What's the Isle of Mohair got to do with Precolombian art?"

"Chichen Itza and Tulum aren't that far away, Rosita," Lucy said. "There's all kinds of Precolombian activity around here. I've got to do my research. Besides, there's some great beaches on the Isla, right, Maggie?"

"Yeah. And maybe my brother's around and he can tell us about where he got the so-called forgeries I sent to New York."

Lucy looked at her. "Maggie, do you still think my consultants in New York were bogus? You know Quentin Washington's reputation."

"Yes, but you saw my pieces. As they say in Waco, them's the real thing, honey."

"I guess we'll just have to track the wild boy down to get to the bottom of this," Lucy said. They entered the terminal and were greeted by a blast of cool air. "Ah, AC," Lucy sighed. "Let's hear it for civilization."

"I hope it's that easy. He's an elusive character," said Maggie.

They rented a VW Bug, strapped the bags on the roof rack, and drove to Punta Sam, where the next car ferry to Isla was an hour away. Passing time drinking beer under a slow-moving ceiling fan in the little pale blue ferry terminal, they watched lizards climb the walls, and the chop-laced sea through unglazed windows. There were no other gringos around; the few visitors who'd selected Isla over the glitzy attractions of Cancún had all gone over from Puerto Juarez, where the passenger ferries plied their trade. "So tell me, Rosita," said Lucy. "What, in the end, did Darren have to say about this trip?"

Rosa took a swallow of beer. "He was okay about it," she said. "Although he wasn't sure why I had to go right now. We had talked about honeymooning in Mexico."

"So you're definitely getting married?" Lucy said. "When we talked the other day you seemed like you weren't so sure. Rosie, that is so great. Did you set a date?"

"No, not exactly, but it'll be this year."

"I tried marriage a couple of times," said Maggie. "Frankly, I prefer dogs to men."

"They are more loyal," said Lucy.

"Hey, I love this guy," said Rosa. "You two are so cynical, I swear to God."

"I've just been burned too many times," said Lucy. "You know that, Rosalita." She covered Rosa's hand with hers, then hoisted her beer bottle. "Here's to you and Darren, bona fide husband material."

"Looks like they're loading," said Maggie. "You ready to roll, ladies?"

At the end of the ferry ride across the eight or nine wind-thrashed miles separating Isla from the mainland, Maggie drove the Bug off the boat. She maneuvered through the narrow streets, dodging taxis, dogs, sailors from the local Mexican Navy base, children, and an assortment of stoned, sunburned northern European men with Jesus hair and eyes that pleaded silently with the three American women as they passed, begging for sex, companionship, or maybe just beer money. Lucy took snapshots of half a dozen of them through the window of the bug. The Blurred German Beggar series. "At least the Isla hasn't been Cancooned," Maggie said as they edged out of town and headed south on the road that hugged the east side of the island. "Still looks like a real village, doesn't it?"

"Complete with an assortment of low-rent hippies," Lucy said. "Just like the good old days." She was happy. The afternoon sky was huge, with enormous puffy clouds posed like abstract white Buddhas against the blue. Sitting in the backseat of a red VW Bug, cruising down a tropical coastline in balmy sunlight, she felt a certain serenity along with her charge of excitement. This was the air she was meant to breathe, and every time she came back to the Caribbean she was reminded of that.

After a few moments they swung left abruptly off the main road onto dirt, entered an inconspicuous grove of trees, and emerged from the thicket to pass through an arched gateway. A tumble-down gate was pushed permanently aside, creating the only opening in a long, faded whitewash wall. "Welcome to South of Carolina," said Maggie, pulling to a stop and turning off the car as three small children dashed out of sight into the bush and two scrawny dogs charged up to the car, barking. Aside from brash dogs and shy children, the Clements compound encompassed a dense abundance of trees and shrubs, a couple of small outbuildings—servant's quarters, it appeared, with dim faces showing in the black holes of unglazed windows—a dozen or so dirt-eating chickens, and, beyond an overgrown tangle of giant pothos, bougainvillea, banana trees, decrepit fountains, and statuary, the red-roofed, white-walled, two-story main house, just barely visible through the unkempt jungle. An old Harley Davidson was parked at the side of the dirt driveway, and the scattered remains of another lay alongside the parking area, among the coconuts and palm branches that had blown down in the wind. Parrots and gulls screamed in the palm trees. "Mama came from South Carolina, and so when Daddy bought her this house that's what she named it," Maggie said as they got out and stretched. "South of Carolina. My goodness, what a ruin. I guess the place just never got over the last hurricane," she added. "Wilma did her slamdance right on top of the Isla, you know."

"But it's so elegantly decayed," said Rosa. "Feels like some demented tyrant from a Marquez novel ought to stagger out here in full dress uniform to address the troops. Only the troops will be chickens, dogs, children, and coconuts."

"And a trio of deranged gringo dames, eh? Is this your brother's bike, Maggie?" Lucy said, checking out the Harley.

"I guess," Maggie said. "Leastwise I know that one is—or was," she added, glancing at the strewn parts. "Looks like he got another. Well, let's go see if anybody's home." Lucy and Rosa followed her as she scattered the chickens, heading down an overgrown tiled pathway toward the house. Off to the right, faces dodged from view as they peered at the dark window holes of the servant's quarters. "They don't seem too happy to see us, do they?" Maggie said dryly. "The 'servants,' I mean."

"Do they know you?" Lucy asked. "They act scared."

"They probably don't recognize me, or maybe it's a new generation, and they don't even know who I am. Once upon a time when I was a kid that was a nice pool," she added sardonically, with a glance at a swimming pool visible beyond the undergrowth. They pushed through for a closer look. The pool, with a naked cherub statue poised on a pedestal at each end, was empty but for a wallow of green slime collected in the deep end. The pool bottom had been tiled with a striking, Moorish-influenced design, still visible through a layer of moss. "Darn, that Nathaniel is really out to lunch, I swear," Maggie said sadly, bitterly. Lucy took out her digital camera and started shooting. This equatorial rot was too good to miss.

"Looks like it once was nice," said Rosa. "Beautiful tile-work, anyway."

"Yes, I guess so," said Maggie. "My mama designed the pattern." She sighed. "She was a talented woman." They all jumped as the natural noise level was abruptly ripped by the blast of a motor starting up in the environs of the house just ahead. It got the dogs barking again. "What in the hell," said Maggie. "Somebody's sure here," she added.

"Sounds like a gas-powered generator to me," said Rosa.

Another layer of noise blasted out over the ratatatat of the generator, and was immediately recognizable. Loud rock n' roll, early seventies variety. "The Rolling Stones!" Lucy cried. "*Exile on Main Street.*"

Maggie pushed the carved mahogany front door open and led the way into a foyer. On the left a formal stair rose to the second story. "Hey, Nate! Natty Boy, you here?" she called over the din. The foyer and the rooms beyond it were empty and felt abandoned, although light spilled in from the other end of the house facing the sea. Lucy, still firing away with her camera, followed Rosa and Maggie through tile-floored, pale pastel rooms strewn with mis-matched furnishings—lacy plantation wicker mixed with heavily formal mahogany antiques. The house appeared uninhabited, although as they passed through a huge dining room, a table strewn with dirty dishes suggested otherwise. Lizards scattered, disappearing into cracks in the walls. Ahead, the Stones rocked on.

A moment later they reached the living room, a grand, two-story volume with a row of wide French doors opening onto an enormous patio facing the sea, with a view ordered by a row of dead palms, their tops starkly bald from hurricane damage. On the patio a blond woman wearing only a brief black bikini bottom and a pair of pink wrap-around sunglasses practiced erotic aerobics on the patio's edge, dramatically framed between two palm trunks, facing the sea.

They observed the woman's writhing rear for a moment, transfixed. Tossing her mane, she danced well, as if she'd put in some time in dance school, or perhaps in a cage dangling over a disco dance floor, or most likely, Lucy decided after a few seconds of watching the pelvic pulsations, peeling scant threads off in a table-dancing joint in Texas, thrusting herself into the faces of gin-drunk entrepreneurs. Gleaming with sweat, she had a tight ass, nine yards of legs, serious muscle definition, and long blond hair with dark roots.

The Stones thrashed, and so did she. Maggie, arms crossed on her chest, cleared her throat. They watched. The woman continued to dance. Lucy walked over to the stereo system, looked over the control panel, and punched a button. The music stopped. The generator rattled on. The woman whirled around. Her breasts turned with her, stiff, unripe, silicone supplemented. "What the fuck!" she snarled, then saw them. "Oh. Whoops." She lifted her sunglasses, and smiled at them. An aging California babe. "Hi." She smiled, came toward them with one hand and two tits outthrust. "I'm Starfish. Sorry I didn't hear you, I was just doing my workout." She had the voice of a child.

Starfish went straight to Maggie, who radiated ruffled authority. "Hello. I'm Margaret. Margaret Clements. This is Rosa Luxemburg, and Lucy Ripken."

"Clements!" she said, ignoring the others. "You must be Nathaniel's sister! Oh, I'm so glad to meet you. Nathaniel's told me all about you," she went on breathlessly, taking both of Maggie's hands. "I had no idea you were going to be coming down."

"Where is Nate—Nathaniel, Miss—"

"Starfish. Just call me Starfish." She giggled. "I changed my name, because I love the ocean so much."

"That's nice, Starfish," said Maggie, extracting her hands. "But where's my brother? You must have come here with him, right?"

"Of course," she said. "How else could I have found this magical place? He's gone on business over to somewhere called Tiki or Taco or something. He said he'd be back in a couple of days, I don't know. Gee," she giggled again. "It's too bad the electricity's gone and everything's falling apart in the house. Otherwise it's a pretty amazing place. The beach is dreamy." She looked out to sea. The imminent arrival of evening had turned the sky a pale shade of lavender. A flock of gulls flew past. Two boats cruised the horizon, where soft clouds had gathered, gold in the fading light. "See what I mean?"

Lucy decided the woman's eyes gave her away. The giggles were disguise. Those icy green eyes revealed the real face. And those hard, pushy tits. Playing seventeen, she was circling forty. Twenty years of that game will turn anybody cold. "I'm sorry," Starfish said. "Lucy, was it?" She offered a hand. Lucy shook it. Her grip was powerful, and tipped with serious, hot red nails. She was not so much muscle-bound as lithe, catlike. "And Rosa?" Another handshake.

"Hullo," said Rosa. "So you dig those walking antiques, the Stones, huh?"

"Oh yeah. Mick is like a god. I met him once." She giggled. "He said I gave the best head in California. 'Course that was a few years back, I must admit, but—" She grinned. "I've only gotten better." She laughed again. The three of them stared at her, appalled. Was she for real? "Gee, if I could only get one of the servants to come in I'd get you some drinks. But ever since Nathaniel left they've been avoiding me. Hey, I know, there's some beers in the cooler. Do you smoke? I have a couple of joints if you're interested."

"Please," said Maggie, her civility stretched by the bare-breasted space cadet. "Don't worry about it. But where is— oh, never mind. We'll get our own bags."

"Bags? You mean you're staying here?" Starfish said.

"This is my family's house, Starf—Mother of God, don't you have a real name?" She was getting pissed. "Of course we're staying here. And maybe if you'd put a shirt on one of the houseboys might show up to help with our bags."

"Hey, take it easy, there's no need to get uptight," Starfish said. She strolled over, picked up a pink tanktop off a wrought iron patio chair, and pulled it on. "I just—Nathaniel wasn't expecting anybody is all. He said nobody else in the family ever came here, so I thought we'd have the place to ourselves."

"Well he was wrong, wasn't he?" Maggie snapped. "Let's go get our things." She strode back through the house. Lucy and Rosa went after her.

"Take it easy, Maggie," said Lucy. "She's harmless, I think."

"Yeah, well, running around with her boobs out like that isn't harmless. The women around here are modest, for God's sake. They're practicing Catholics! Who the hell does she think she is!" She mimicked the giggle. "God, Nathaniel's had some trailer-trash girlfriends in his time, but this one tops them all."

"Those tits look hard as coconuts, don't they?" said Lucy. "I wonder where they were manufactured."

Rosa said, "God, where did she come from? And more important, when is she going?"

"As soon as I find Nate," said Maggie. "Meanwhile, the bedrooms, such as they may be, are upstairs. Let's unload our stuff, and maybe now that the bimbo's got her boobs under wraps I can rouse a little help to go buy some fish for dinner."

Lucy woke at dawn. Bedding down on a thin stack of blankets on a tile floor made the early wake up inevitable, but regardless of that, the allure of the pale light gently pulled her up to consciousness. She got to her feet, carefully slipping out from between Rosa and Maggie. They had slept in a row on the floor in a bedroom that once was shared, then fought over, by Maggie and Nathaniel. Starfish occupied the other seaside room, the master bedroom that once belonged to the parents and now contained the only remaining bed, post-Wilma. Lucy slipped on a one-piece swimsuit and a pair of shorts, grabbed her digital camera, and tiptoed quietly downstairs and out onto the front porch. The sun lifted through banks of clouds over the sea to the east, bathing the decaying old house in a sweet glow, rose-tinted gold at the heart of a blue-gray morning. The high tide surf danced along the sandy beach, where a few shorebirds ran. Lucy put down the camera, pulled off her shorts, and dashed into the lapping waves. She dove, and impulsively peeled her suit off as she streamed through the salt sea. Warm dawn water felt best on naked skin. She surfaced, threw her suit up on the sand, and dove back in. She did the crawl for 500 strokes out to sea, then reversed direction, turned over and backstroked shoreward, watching the mobile etchings of bird silhouettes, black against the pale blue of morning sky overhead.

She didn't stop until her backstroking hand hit bottom in the shallows near shore; then she turned over and floated, catching her breath. The sun had burned off the clouds, and now warmed the house with direct light. She caught a glint of reflection, and realized someone had come out onto the patio and picked up her camera. She waved, assuming it was Rosa or Maggie; after all the tequila and reefer Starfish had consumed before, during, and after dinner, no way it could be her.

But it was Ms. Fish, Lucy realized, as the woman rose from a crouch and came down to the water's edge, where the light snared her golden hair. Starfish, in her pink tank-top and a pair of warm-up pants, was playing with a very expensive toy: Lucy's camera. Lucy swam closer. "Hi," she said. "You're up early."

"I'm always up early," Starfish said. "I like to go in the water before the sun gets too high, while the moon vibes are lingering. I'm a Pisces, you know, with a Cancer moon and a lot of planets in Scorpio. Heavily into water, you know."

"Yeah, well, that camera's not into water at all," Lucy said, "so please be careful." The woman was holding it by the neckstrap very casually. She slung it up.

"Oh, I'm sorry. Don't worry." She smiled. "You want me to take a picture of you?" She looked over at Lucy's suit, lying on the sand, and Lucy, who had forgotten that she was naked in the water, remembered.

"Nude? No thanks," Lucy said, treading in the shallows. "But if you'll hold on a minute, I'll get dressed and we'll do some pictures of you. The light is perfect." She stood up and ran for her suit.

"That sounds like fun," said Starfish, pointing the camera and firing off one shot as Lucy dashed past.

"Hey, I thought I told you no nude shots," Lucy said, jumping into her suit.

"Sorry," Starfish smiled. "I couldn't resist." She came over and proffered the camera with a smile. "You have such a wonderful body," she added huskily. In spite of the sun-baked skin, she looked softer and better in morning light, without makeup—a fortyish child-woman, pretty faced with a lift to preserve it and a mane of bleached locks to frame it. But the compliment and the look that came with it added up to a come on, and Lucy knew it. Lucy took the camera, slipped the strap over her head, and looked at Starfish through the lens.

"Well, no harm, since it's mine to delete. So, you want to do some more dancing, or dive, or—hey, why don't you start by doing some warm-ups, you know, just like you would if you were getting ready to perform. Great," she said, as Starfish, needing no coaxing, leaped up on the low patio wall, the attentive camera transforming her. She went into a kind of Egypto-erotic dance step, moving down the wall in a stylized prance. At the corner of the patio she whirled back to face Lucy, who was firing away, and suddenly pulled her shirt off over her head. She was pretty hot stuff, Lucy had to admit, watching the dancing Starfish through the camera. Lucy held the camera a foot away from her face in the new digital mode of image-making, as Starfish writhed back along the wall, abandoning the Egyptian moves for a more straight-on sexual dance. She leaped off the wall onto the beach, undid the drawstring of her pants, and stepped out of them. Naked, she shook her hair back, raised her arms into the sun, and slowly lifted a leg and twisted herself into an elegant, birdlike yoga pose. Lucy circled around her, shooting her body in the golden light.

The camera shut itself down. "Damn," Lucy said. "I gotta get a new battery. Gimme a minute." She ran for the house, found her camera bag, quickly changed the batteries, then went back outside.

Starfish had seated herself in the sand and assumed full lotus position, facing the morning sun with her legs crossed and her hands open in her lap. Her eyes were closed. Lucy took a closer look at her weathered face. There was character there—a measure of sorrow, and some hard-earned peace, she thought, reflected in the grace of the lotus. The yoga looked effortless. There was more to this woman than plastic boobs.

Lucy photographed her in profile, then moved around front. "Yoga brings me back to myself," Starfish said softly. "I get so lost sometimes." The little girl voice was gone. Lucy continued to shoot. "My real name's Isabel. Isabel Chapin. I used to dance in the San Francisco ballet when I was a girl. Then I discovered LSD and that was that," she finished matter of factly, and opened her eyes. "Have you ever met Nathaniel? Margaret's brother?" Lucy shook her head as Starfish—Isabel—stood up and stretched. "He's—I don't know what Margaret's like, she doesn't seem to care much for me, but Nate's a real sad guy. I mean, he's a lot of fun, we love to party together, but just about every time he gets drunk he. . . . Did she tell you about their mom?"

"Just that she died," Lucy said softly, still shooting as Isabel picked up her tank top and pulled it on.

"Well, the story he tells me, when he's had a few shots of Sauza Conmemorativo and maybe a joint or two to top it off, is all about finding her. How he found her dead from an overdose." She put on her warm-up pants. Every move was camera conscious.

"Jesus. Where was she?"

"He was eleven years old. She had taken, like, twenty reds, and he found her passed out naked on a bathroom floor. Margaret was away at college, and the old man away on business. Thing was, she wasn't dead when he found her. So he hauled her into the bedroom, and then he got to watch her die before the ambulance got there."

"My God. Pretty traumatic, I'd say," said Lucy.

"Well, we all have 'em," said Isabel, "but his seems worse than most, doesn't it?"

"Yeah."

"He's still getting misery mileage out of it, I'll tell you that. Blaming Big Bad Dad. But don't get me wrong, me and Nathaniel have a good time, in spite of all that. So what about you and those two?" she said with a glance back at the house.

"We're just friends."

"You've known Margaret awhile?"

"No, just a few days."

"She's—"

"A rich woman."

Isabel smiled. "Right. That's what it is. That attitude, I mean. She's rich. So you just met and she decided to invite you down to the family estate that she hasn't visited in ten years."

"Something like that," Lucy said. "Actually, we're looking for Nathaniel."

"Why's that?"

"He sounds like an intriguing character."

"Oh, he's that all right, but that's not why you came here, I bet, is it?"

"I came for the waters," Lucy said. "What about you? I mean, how long have you and Nathaniel been hanging out?"

"Oh, I've known Nate for years," she said. "We go in and out of it—being fuck-buddies, I mean. Usually it's when one or the other of us is busted up and broken-hearted over somebody or other. Right now we're in it." She smiled. "I know you think I sound cheap, but I'm just blunt, honey, just plain blunt." The look held a challenge.

"Whatever you say, Isabel. So what are you guys doing here, anyways?"

"Hey, it was cold in L.A., raining in Texas, and Nathaniel had some business to do. So here I am."

"What kind of business?"

"None of yours." She grinned. "Or of mine, for that matter. I don't really know. He's got his hand in a lot of different deals, know what I mean?"

"Not really."

"Well, imagine if you were born rich, lived the high life, then got cut off without a nickel at the age of twenty-five. What would you do?"

"I haven't a clue. Not having been born rich makes it hard to imagine."

"Well, try. Let's just say he's done what he's had to. He should be making a living playing horn, he plays the hell out of the tenor sax, but he's never gone after it professionally."

"Hey, Luce," said Rosa, wandering across the patio sleepily. "How'd you sleep? Morning, uh, Starfish."

"Hi," Starfish said, back in baby talk mode. Isabel had gone away. "Me and Lucy were just talkin'. You wanna go swimmin' with me?"

"Badly, of course," said Lucy. "I always sleep badly. You know that."

After morning ablutions Lucy and Rosa drove off to town, leaving Maggie to reacquaint herself with the workings of the "staff" and the house, and to get to know the brother's girlfriend. They parked the Bug and walked the streets for half an hour, while the compulsive shopper Rosa determined that there was nothing she needed to buy on Isla Mujeres except a cup of coffee and a piece of toast. Then Lucy led the way to Playa Norte, the palm-lined north beach, sheltered from the east wind by the graceless hulk of the overscale hotel some greedy idiot developer had stuck on top of the beautiful little saltwater lagoon on the northeast tip of the island. From there the beach swung west in a lazy concave curve. The whitecaps indicated the wind was blasting at sea, but the sheltered shallows were tranquil. Groups of long-haired tourists—more dazed Germans and their fräuleins—cavorted in the water near the jalapa hotel, where you could rent a hut and a hammock for a few bucks a day. The girls went topless there and all along the Playa Norte, and most of the locals stayed away.

"God this is so beautiful," said Rosa as they strolled—rather quickly through the scorching hot sand—down to the water's edge and headed east. Lucy had her eye on a sailboard a hundred yards ahead. Lying just above the water line, fully rigged, it looked like a log, a longboard, but she was dying to get out there into the breeze. The water was 82 degrees, the air five degrees warmer, and 20 knots of wind blew outside the shelter of the cove.

The owner of the sailboard turned out to be a slender Mexican boy-man in his late twenties, wearing a tiny leopardskin swimsuit and a sharktooth on a silver chain. His easy grin showed off a silver canine fang, left of center, planted to glitter among two healthy rows of white teeth. He introduced himself as José and his young friend as Rodrigo. José was thin but muscular, with reddish sun-bleached hair and the inimitable style of a beachboy gigolo tourist-fucker. He cased them both thoroughly while Lucy negotiated the rental of the sailboard. José took Lucy's ten dollars American in advance and had Rodrigo, gigolo-in-training, drag it down to the water.

Lucy climbed on, uphauled the sail, and took off, slowly at first and then with a burst of speed as she cleared the cove and hit open water, where the white chop had indicated a good strong blow, enough to get the waterlogged board moving at a fair clip. She tacked downwind a while, did a slow-motion jibe maybe half a mile offshore, and dropped the sail once she was facing back toward the beach. She sat down on the board, legs dangling in the warm water, and had a look shoreward. She rocked with the rolling swells, and picked out the ants that were Rosa, José, and Rodrigo, standing at the water's edge. Even from half a mile offshore, she could read the insistent body English of José making his moves on resistant Rosa. Maybe she shouldn't have left Rosa to fend off the bad boy on her own for too long. Rosa could be a sucker for the wrong guy sometimes. But Darren was supposed to have cured her of that.

Lucy did a few more tacks up and down the bay; while the soggy log of a board got moving in this restless wind, it didn't have enough spark to really jam, and so she got sidetracked. There was much to think about, from Rosa and Darren to Margaret, and brother Nathaniel, off in Tiki or Taco, said Starfish. It had to be Ticul she meant. Ticul, where Gutierrez cooked up his fakes.

Lucy sailed in, suddenly conscious of sunburn on her shoulders. She'd greased up with number 40 waterproof, but it did wear off after a while. Cancer lurked offshore, or rather overhead, waiting to pounce with ultraviolet death rays. How odd to fear the sun. It was a feeling she would never get used to.

She kicked the daggerboard up a few yards off shore, and stepped down into ankle-deep water. Rodrigo splashed out to fetch the board. Up on dry sand, Rosa stood with her arms crossed stiffly, listening to José's line.

"So how was it, baby?" José barked at Lucy, flashing his silver-tooth smile. "Pretty good wind out there, yes?"

"Not bad," Lucy said. "But that's a slug you're sailing, man. You oughta at least get a new sail. I mean, if you can't afford a new board, too."

"Hey, she works okay," he said. "You just have to get used to her. Leave it there, baby," he called out to Rodrigo. "I'll show you, eh?" he said, with a glance at Rosa. "Show Miss Rosa here how it is done." He trotted down to the water, where Rodrigo handed him the mast. He turned the board around and walked it into the sea.

"Take it away, José," Lucy said. He grinned and waved at them as he sailed off, holding the boom with one hand. "So was he hot to trot, or what?"

"Yeah. He's definitely a horny dog," Rosa said. "And gets to the point pretty damned fast, too."

"Well, that's what dogs do," said Lucy. "Cut to the butt, sniff, and try to hump."

"Well, I'll tell you who he has humped," Rosa said. "Our friend Starfuck."

"Starfish? He knows Starfish?" Lucy said.

"Biblically, as they say," Rosa said. "And knows Nathaniel—the party gringo, he called him—as well."

"Jesus. Those two are loose, eh?"

"Well, I don't know about Nathaniel, but according to José there," Rosa said, nodding seaward, where they watched as the beach boy flipped his sailboard up on one rail and cruised along, crouching on the other, "she showed up a couple of days before Nathaniel got here, in the company of two 'very sleek gringo dudes.' Then as soon as Nathaniel showed up, she started hanging with him. And then when they connected, it turned out that Nathaniel knew these guys, and had planned to meet them, and she pretended she'd never seen them before."

"José saw all this?"

"It happened right here."

"Sounds like they had a plan."

"But why would she pretend not to know them when Nathaniel showed up?"

"Good question, Rosita Conchita," Lucy said. "To which you and I shall find the answer. But when did Tarzan there get his licks, pardon the phrasing, in on Starfish, anyway?"

"Last couple of days, since Nathaniel took off with the two so-called sleek dudes."

"Nice work, Rosita, finding all that out. How'd you do it?"

"A twitch of the hips gets you a lot of mileage with a dickhead like that," she said, looking out to sea, where José capered on his sailboard. "He is definitely eager to please."

"Yeah, right," Lucy said. "But you're practically a married woman. You're not supposed to play those games anymore."

"Not yet, I'm not," Rosa said. "Besides, this is kind of fun. So what's next, Sherlock?"

Given that the island's only luxury hotel, the hulking El Presidente on the lagoon, was bankrupt and roofless thanks to Wilma, "next" meant figuring out which other island hotels ranked highest on the luxe scale, and visiting them. After all, where else would "two sleek gringo dudes" stay on Isla Mujeres? They hit paydirt on the third one, a two-story sky blue building on the ocean side of the island called the Boca Caribe. Not exactly luxe, but respectable. Lucy approached the desk clerk and explained that she'd arrived three days later than she was supposed to, and had her friend Starfish or Isabel Chapin checked in or out recently? Blonde woman, strong, grande—Lucy held her hands out in front of her chest, grinning. The man smirked, reddening, oh yes, she was here. And two gentlemen with her? I cannot give out this information, sorry. Lucy slipped a ten-dollar bill onto the counter; the man glanced around, took the bill, then turned the registration book so she could read it, and she quickly found Chapin's name—Starfish was apparently for stage and screen use only—written in a week back. Directly above her name, two guys named Jack Partridge and Lewis Mon, who listed Ft. Worth, Texas, as their hometown, were checked in and checked out the same days as Chapin.

Lucy and Rosa headed out in search of a telephone. They found one on the wall in the Kentucky Fried Bar, downtown Isla. The Eagles played "Hotel California" on the sound system, and three besotted American dudes sat at a table in the dark and otherwise empty room with a fifth of tequila, bottles of beer, shot glasses, salt shakers, and sliced lemons spread out on the tabletop. They stared at Lucy and Rosa, in their bathing suits, sandals, and shorts, with the eyes of men who had been at sea too long. Lucy did the international operator shuffle, and finally got connected with New York City. Harold was not at home. She left a message: "Harry, need some help. Can you see if there's anything I should know about Jack Partridge, like the bird, or Lewis Mon, L-e-w-i-s-M-o-n, anywhere in the wonderful world of files you can access? Wire me a reply to AmEx, Cancún. All's well, talk to you soon."

Then she stood close by and pretended not to listen as Rosa called Darren, and pretended not to notice the three drunk gringo sailors leering at her legs. "Hi, Darren," Rosa said, and paused. "Yes," Rosa said. "No," Rosa said. "A couple of days," Rosa said. "No, he wasn't. Yeah. His girlfriend. Yes. Weird woman named Starfish. Spacey. Off to find

Nathaniel. Tiki? Ticul. Yeah. Ticul." A longer pause. "Really? Jesus, that's creepy."

"Let's go, Rosa," Lucy whispered, tapping the face of her watch and catching Rosa's eye. "Margaret's expecting us back for lunch." Throwing a glance at the brain-damaged drunks, she raised her voice: "And these bozos are beginning to get on my nerves. Where're your manners, boys?" she asked them as Rosa hung up the phone with a fast gottagogoodbye to Darren. "Lost at sea?"

"Hey, baby," one of them slurred as Lucy and Rosa beat it out the door. "Wanna party?"

Lucy ignored him. "So how's the affianced one?" She said to Rosa.

"Oh, he's all right," Rosa said, but she didn't look happy. "He just wants me home."

"Can he wait a few days, I hope?" Lucy said. She didn't want to lose Rosa. Not now, with things just getting interesting.

"I guess." She looked tense. "Hey, you know what? That cop Rodriguez called. He told Darren those guys both committed suicide."

"Suicide?" Lucy did a doubletake. "What?"

"Yeah. Both of 'em OD'ed on phenobarbitol. Injected intravenously. The needle marks were there, and insanely high levels of dope in their blood."

"He's got to be kidding. So how'd they get in the pool?"

"Shot up and jumped in, I guess. Darren didn't say if Rodriguez told him." She looked solemn. "But he did say they were HIV positive."

"AIDS? Both of them? Christ, those poor—"

"No, not AIDS. Just HIV positive. They weren't sick. There's a difference, you know?"

"Yeah, I know. Some of my best friends are HIV positive, and they're still alive. That's the difference."

"Well, apparently the authorities in Santa Fe consider it reason enough to commit suicide."

"That's a crock of bullshit," said Lucy, shaking her head angrily as they approached the red rentabug. "I'd bet a million bucks somebody put that dope in them—somebody with a stake in this art scam." They climbed in, and Lucy drove as they headed back to South of Carolina. "You saw their house, their life. Those guys had too much going for them, HIV or not."

Rosa folded her arms across her chest, and sank in her seat. She looked weary, and it was not yet noon. "Yeah, well, who would you suggest as the culprit, Lucy?" Rosa asked. "Where are the bad guys?"

"I don't know, Rosita. I don't fucking know. But just hearing that line about suicide pissed me off is all. Those lame cops. Gays. AIDS. Death. They just line them up and knock them over like dominoes. The stupid fools with their ignorant assumptions!"

They found Maggie in the kitchen with two Mexican women. She watched over them as they cleaned up, chatting in fluent Spanish. "Hey, girls," she said. "Just catching up on ten years of local gossip. How's town? Starfish find you?"

"No. Was she looking?" Lucy asked.

"Said she was going riding. Took the Harley, headed that way, said she was gonna look for you on the beach."

"We were there, and she wasn't." Lucy shrugged. "What's up?"

"Well, I thought we could eat lunch and maybe catch a ferry, head up toward Ticul and see if we can track down Nate. You ever been to Chichen Itza? It's worth seeing. We can spend the night there, catch the ruins at dawn, and then go on to Ticul." She lapsed back into Spanish with the help, and Lucy turned to Rosa.

"Okay with you?"

"Sure." They followed Maggie into the dining room, where the table had been set up for three with heavy, elegant old flatware and silver. "So yeah, let's hit the ruins, Maggie," Lucy said. "I just gotta make a quick trip to the AmEx office in Cancún if it's not too far out of the way."

"What about Starfish?" Rosa said.

"What about her?" said Maggie. "She was here when we got here, no doubt she'll be here when we get back. Like the critter she's named herself for, we'll probably have to pry her loose to move her. Nate has an occasional penchant for airhead bimbos, so she's no surprise. It'll be interesting to see what he has to say about her."

They ate a great lunch of fresh local cod cooked Veracruzana style, with black beans and tortillas on the side, drank coffee instead of beer, and threw their bags into the Bug for another ferry ride. Maggie had imposed some discipline on the premises; by the time they left half a dozen men and women were cleaning up the house and yard, and someone had re-connected the electricity. There was no sign of Starfish as they drove off.

The trip into Cancún yielded a telegram from Harry. BE CAREFUL STOP THE BIRD IS A VERY BAD ONE STOP FILE A MILE DEEP STOP SAME FOR LM BE CAREFUL LUCY I LOVE YOU STOP I LOVE YOU STOP DONT DO ANYTHING FOOLISH STOP THESE ARE CAREER BAD GUYS STOP BEWARE STOP LOVE HARRY PS CALL ME AGAIN SOON IM HERE FOR YOU LOVE YOU STOP HARRY. Lucy read it twice, thought, what am I getting into here?, then stuffed it into her pocket, jumped back into the backseat of the car, and said, "Let's roll, cuties."

"What's the word?" Rosa asked over her shoulder.

"Oh, nothing," Lucy said. "Just some business with my editor."

The two-lane paved road running inland from the coast lay flat and straight for miles. The terrain, too, was flat, and the dense forest obscured everything beyond the immediate edges of the road. In Lucy, at least, this created an oddly claustrophobic feeling of being closed in beneath, and in spite of, the immensity of the sky. Every now and then a small sign indicated a dirt road or a trail to a settlement, but they couldn't see beyond the trees to get a sense of where the trails led. Occasionally they passed small groups of short, mysterious-looking men carrying long rifles, walking along the roadside. Maggie said they were Mayan deer hunters. To Lucy's eyes, their dark-eyed, high-cheekboned faces, their pitch-black hair and dark skin, and their short, compact forms appeared to have emerged from ancient history.

Eventually they drove through the town of Vallodolid, and soon reached Chichen Itza, where they stopped for the night at the old, sedately raffish, yellow, two-story hotel in the archaeological park on the edge of the ruins. The huge trees along the driveway and around the porte cochere were full of screaming birds. They entered a lobby that appeared to be suspended in time, a mausoleum of elegant history, with ceiling fans turning in slow motion over faded wicker and tile floors, and the jungle stretching snaky tendrils in and around the windowframes. The hotel's general manager, Señor Herman Gomez, was a friend of Maggie's father. A few moments after she gave her name to the desk clerk, perched alone and forlorn behind thirty yards of ancient mahogany countertop, the GM emerged, an old man slowly shuffling, and after greeting Maggie with courtly grace and kissing each of their hands with his dry cool lips as they were introduced, he explained that no, he had not seen Nathaniel in many months. Then he showed them to the Presidential Suite, where they each had a bedroom with a private bath. There were three new hotels down the road, with color TV and bars built into the swimming pools and discos that throbbed till dawn, and they were full of Club Med heads up from Cancún to do a little ruin-hopping the next day between parties. This hotel, on the other hand, was old and elegant, with valleys in the beds and a recalcitrant hot water tap in Lucy's bathtub. The women shared a quiet dinner as the roaring of the jungle rose to meet the fall of night. There were three other tables occupied by ancient American tourists in the long, dark dining room, with maybe two dozen tables empty, and not a soul at the bar except the bartender, who looked like he might be Herman Gomez's older brother. No, he had not seen Nathaniel either. After a taste of brandy they went to bed early, planning a hike through the ruins at dawn.

Instead, light-sleeping Lucy stayed up most of the night listening to the archaeological Sound and Light Spectacular blazing and blasting through the Mayan jungle. A combination of lasers and primitivo-disco beat, the spectacle drew a crowd of Cancún tourist yuppies who partied at the foot of the Temple of the Warrior till the wee hours, when at last they dispersed in a small fleet of buses back to their own hotels. At six, when Rosa knocked on her door, Lucy had been asleep for an hour or two. The three of them gathered in the restaurant to drink coffee and eat boiled eggs. Neither of the other women had even been aware of the Chichen Itza Sound and Light Spectacular. And so Lucy dragged along behind as they wandered the ruins for three hours. She was properly impressed with the ball court, where the players, it was surmised, attempted to hit the ball through a tiny loop way up high on a stone wall. Supposedly they were not allowed to use their hands. Was it the winners or the losers who were honored with decapitation? Or was it that they were dragged off to the chac mool atop the Temple of Kukulcan and had their still-beating hearts cut out? Or were they instead herded down to the Cenote, the sacred well, weighted down with gold, and tossed in? When she tired she grew morbid. Couldn't be helped.

Off to Ticul, in pursuit of the elusive Nathaniel. The trip occupied most of the day, since they elected to drive up to Merida and double back, sticking to main roads rather than

braving one of the dirt tracks that covered the territory between Kantunil and Tekit. Lucy nodded off sporadically in
the backseat, and thus felt slightly revived by the time they
arrived in Ticul around nightfall.

They drove into the middle of Ticul and parked just off
the plaza behind the church. While strolling across the
plaza they heard, mingling with the chatter of families out
on evening promenade and the rumble and honk of passing cars and the perfectly pitched cries of sellers of corn,
popsicles, tamales, tacos, helados, and other edible items,
the unmistakable wail of a tenor saxophone. "It's Nate,"
Maggie said. "Listen." They paused, and heard twelve closing bars of nitty gritty blues, followed by a pause that was
then followed by a hot Mexican polka, the sax playing
lead. The rollicking sound led them a block off the plaza.
They dodged the pedicabs and triciclos, turning right on
Calle Merida to stop outside the Villa Maya Restaurant,
with a neon pyramid lighting up the sign. Behind an
adobe wall, they could hear the band cutting loose on the
patio; wailing over all, the sound of the sax. "That's Nate,"
said Maggie. "I could tell that fat tone from a million miles
away. Let's go in. You first. Find a table so I can keep my
back to him. When he comes over to say hello, I want to
surprise him."

"What makes you think he's going to come and greet
us?" Rosa asked.

"Oh, don't worry about that," Maggie said, pulling
open a faded blue wooden door. They followed her into
the restaurant patio. "Soon as he sees you he'll be over."

The women quickly took seats at a table under the open sky. The band commenced with another tune as Lucy ordered beers and they sat back to listen.

The band members were all Mexican except Nathaniel: two guitarists, an accordionist, a bass, a drummer, a trumpet player, and a fiddle player. The tune was another polka, tempo-wise, but too jazzy to call it that. Nathaniel was remaking the music even as they played it, pulling in elements of R & B, quoting Coltrane, circling the beat to land on it one time, close by the next. A master at work.

Lucy looked him over. Nathaniel Clements was about six feet tall. He wore old jeans and a black T-shirt and appeared very thin. He had medium-long blond hair pushed back behind his ears, and a clean-shaven face shaped like his sister's. Lucy didn't have to look hard to tell that he was a handsome man, in spite of the tension that distorted his jaw as he worked the mouthpiece. He wore sunglasses in the falling darkness, so they could not see his eyes, but Lucy sensed that they would be blue and full of clouds, like Maggie's. A lit cigarette stuck out sideways from the neck of his horn, where he'd wedged it, and smoke drifted up in irregular patterns as the voluptuously curved tenor danced intensely, driven by Nathaniel's obsessive body English. Swaying and bobbing like a mad bird, he appeared possessed by his own music.

But this dancing did nothing to diminish his cool. In Lucy's eyes, for that moment at least, Nathaniel Clements's cool existed beyond diminishing, untouchable, Platonic; gleaming horn in hand, he embodied the principle of cool.

Lucy did something she hadn't done in years. Within five minutes of sitting down, as the band wrapped up the tune, she pictured herself in bed with a man she didn't even know. What was with her and ex-junkies, dopers, and borderline bad boys? She didn't have more than a few seconds to wonder. Sure enough, as soon as the band finished, he picked them out, set his sax down on a stand, and headed over to their table, removing his sunglasses en route.

"Evening, ladies," he said, sauntering up. His Texas accent was much heavier than his sister's. "Ah hope you enjoyed the—Maggie!" he cried, interrupting himself as he spotted his older sis. "What the hell. I can't believe it!" he said as Maggie stood up and they hugged. "Jesus in a jumpsuit! Where did you all come from? How did you find me here?"

"Hey, bro," Maggie said. "You leave tracks like a tank." They stood back and looked each other over, smiling. "Bub, you ever gonna look your age? Look at this baby face." She offered him to the other women. "Nate, I want you to meet a coupla friends of mine. This is Rosa Luxemburg." Rosa half-rose, they shook hands, said hellos. "And this is Lucy, Lucy Ripken. She's come all the way from New York City. And you know why she's come, Nate?" Maggie said, cutting right to the heart of the matter as Lucy stood for a handshake.

"Hey, not now, Maggie," Lucy said quickly. She wanted to size the situation up a little before plunging in. "Hi, Nate. Nice to meet you." She shook his hand, had a better look at his face. Maggie was right to wonder if he would ever catch up to his own years—he looked eighteen, although his eyes were guarded and distant behind the softly maniacal afterglow left by the music. There was something unformed and yet dangerous in his face, some weakness. A perpetual adolescent. She'd known a few. Lucy quickly guessed that he grew up only when he picked up the horn, and maybe as well when he put down a few drinks.

"Likewise, Lucy Ripken," he said, grinning. Clearly he'd figured out who was cruising here. "But what's the story, Mags? You girls down here to party, or what?"

"Siddown, Nate," said Maggie. He did, next to Lucy, then pulled out a Camel and lit it. He smoked in the old guilt-free style, like a French movie star imitating James Dean.

"Bring us a round of beers," he called to a passing waiter. "And a shot of Sauza for me, Jaime," he added. "Any of you ladies want tequila?" he asked quickly. "I like to do a shot or two between sets. Keeps the improvisational fires stoked."

"Nah," said Rosa. "Stuff's too intense for me."

"I'll have one," Lucy said. "Hey, that was some serious horn you were playing there."

"Thanks. I try to get a few licks in where I can. These guys are amazing." He gestured at the band members milling around near the stage. "I can throw anything at 'em, and they pick it right up and roll with it. Bring me another shot, eh?" he added as the waiter arrived and put beers and a single shot of tequila, along with lemon and salt, on the table. "This one's for the lady, here," he added, smiling at Lucy as he pushed the shot glass her way. The guy was definitely charming, although the "lady" talk would wear thin fast, Lucy decided.

"Thanks," she said. "So how'd you end up in a band down here, for God's sake?"

"Well, you folks probably came from the Isla, right? I mean, I don't know what y'all're up to down here, but I figure Mags here musta showed you the house."

"And the broad," Maggie finished for him. "And the mess. And the dead motorcycle. Jesus, Nate, when are you gonna—"

"Hey, don't start in with your bullshit, Maggie. Gimme a break. Star's an old friend."

"Yeah, well, you guys coulda done a little better with SOC, Nate," Maggie said. "The place is a ruin, for God's sake!"

"Well, what the fuck!" He came right back at her. "What's it been? Ten years since you were there? What the hell do you care, Maggie?"

"Hey, hey," Lucy cut in. "Come on, cut the bickering. Jesus. We're not here to argue housekeeping, for God's sake!"

"Sorry," Maggie said, but the edge remained in her voice. "Sorry. Look, let's cut the bullshit. Nathaniel, Lucy came to Santa Fe because she says the pieces I sent to New York—the ones you brought across the border to me— were fakes. That's why we're here. So what do you have to say to that?"

"Fakes?" he said, and Lucy noted his eyes sneak a glance across the room. "What are you talking about?" His disbelief seemed credulous, as far as she could tell. But then again, he had the look of a polished liar. No telling, really.

"Some friends of mine in the business of knowing this stuff had a look at them, and think they're fake," Lucy said.

"But another expert said they were okay," Rosa interjected.

"So here I am, trying to figure it out. Actually, I'm writing a story about it," Lucy said. "I thought maybe you could tell me where you got the pieces."

"Wait a minute, slow down," Nate said, and Lucy stole a glance where his eyes had gone. Two American men in pale suits, and a dark-haired woman, facing away, sat at a corner table across the room, eating dinner. "So are you telling me I—my sources sold me fakes or not?"

"Maybe, baby," said Maggie.

"Yes," said Lucy. "Some of them are definitely forgeries."

"Whoa," said Maggie. "Just a minute, Lucy. Nothing is that clear now, is it?"

"As a matter of fact, it is," Lucy said quietly. "I was in the gallery in New York when Quentin and Beth Washington, some friends of mine who happen to be experts in the field, examined the pieces you sent. Quentin said they were definitely fake. There was no doubt about it. I can't speak for your two pieces, but the New York stuff is bogus." Lucy picked up her shot of tequila, ate some salt, downed the shot, then finished with a bite of lemon. "Whew!" she gasped.

"Well," said Nathaniel after a few seconds had passed. "What the hail." He grinned at Maggie, putting on the drawl. "So what am Ah s'posed ta do, Sis? There ain't no money-back guarantees in this biz, far as I know." With that he licked up some salt, knocked back his own shot of tequila, and bit a slice of lemon. He took the peel out of his mouth and grinned again. The grin faded as two men, both elegantly dressed in pale tropical suits without ties, appeared at the table. "Hey, boys," Nate said. His tone was still relaxed, but Lucy read fear in his eyes. "How ya doin'? Ladies, this here's some friends of mine down from Texas—Louie Mon and Jack Partridge. Boys, like you to meet my sis, Margaret—Maggie—and a couple friends a hers."

Greetings were spoken. Mon was fiftyish and paunchy; Partridge thirtysomething, slick, black-haired, and utterly self-assured. Their clothes were expensive. Lucy looked them over obliquely but carefully. They hardly looked at her. Partridge, in another life, might be her type, but not this time around. The other guy looked like a league bowler with a good tailor. Harry had called them professional bad guys. Nothing in their eyes or demeanor suggested a threat. She wondered what bad they did. "Well," said Nate, after the brief exchange of vapid pleasantries. Maggie was tense, and it was obvious to all. Erratic siblings can do that. "I'd ask you to join us, boys, but I got another set to play. You ladies gonna stick around awhile, maybe we can get together afterwards. I know another bar where this mariachi band just kicks ass."

"I don't think so, Nate. We've been up since dawn and I'm exhausted. But we need to talk about the—that other thing, some more," Maggie said.

"Yeah, right." He grinned too easily at Mon and Partridge. "Family affairs, boys, you know," he said, then returned his attention to his sister. "I'm stayin' at the Parc

Azul Hotel. It's right around the corner. Room seventeen. Come by in the mornin' and we'll get some breakfast and have a chat." He looked at Lucy. "You sure you don't wanna stick around a while? The next set's gonna smoke. I'd love to have another drink with you afterwards."

"Sounds good to me," Lucy said. "Rosa?"

"Excuse me," interjected a smiling Lewis Mon. "But we have some business to take care of, Nathaniel. Immediately after the set, I mean."

"Right," Nate said. "Well, stick around for a couple tunes anyway, huh?"

"Hey, Nathaniel," a guitar player called out from the stage. "Show time, my friend."

"Gotta go," Nate said. "See you tomorrow, Maggie." He dashed for the stage.

"I think I will hang here for a little while," Lucy said, although she was running on alcohol and not much else.

"I'm gonna cash it in," said Maggie, rising. "The Parc Azul, did he say? Maybe we'll check in there too. Rosa, are you coming?"

"Yeah, I think so," Rosa said. "Sorry, Lucy, I can't do it." She stood and smiled at the two men, who didn't seem to have much to say. "Nice to meet you all." She and Maggie left.

"Well," said Lucy, getting up. "Hope to see you again, gents. I'm gonna hang out at the bar. Goodnight." She gave Mon and Partridge a smile, they nodded, pleasantly if noncommittally, in response, and Lucy headed into the restaurant. She went to the bar, ordered a beer, then swiveled around to watch and listen as the band started up again.

Nate blew a blast on the horn, approached a mike, and said, "Good evening, ladies and gentlemen. Thanks for coming to listen. We're the Temple Dogs, and we play what you want to hear. This first tune is an original I wrote for the band. It's called 'Precolombian Jive.'" He snapped his fingers, a bass line snaked in, and the tune took off.

About forty-five minutes through the set—during which Nate downed three more shots of tequila and three bottles of beer, and it only improved his phenomenal saxophone playing—Lucy slipped out the patio door and walked around the corner toward the plaza. On the way out, she noticed that Mon and Partridge were still there, in their corner table on the other side of the room, although the woman who'd been sitting with them had left. On the plaza she found a taxi; she climbed in, and as they pulled around the corner she explained to the driver what she wanted. This was a long shot but worth a try.

Lucy woke with a start as the driver, Eduardo, whispered at her, "Excuse me, miss, but I theenk the men you have described come out now." She looked up. Sure enough, Nathaniel and the two pale-suited goons headed down the sidewalk away from the blue door of the Villa Maya.

"Follow, but slowly, slowly," Lucy said softly, forcing her weary brain onto red alert. Eduardo started up and crept along, around the corner, where the three men unlocked and entered a dark-blue late-model American car. Nathaniel's awkward lurch into the backseat suggested the beer and tequila had caught up to him. The younger one, Jack Partridge, drove the car, and they quickly headed out of downtown and hooked onto Route 184. Lucy and Eduardo stayed sufficiently back, a green taxi in thin traffic, to go unnoticed. She hoped.

A few miles outside town the blue car, a few hundred yards ahead, abruptly turned off onto a dirt driveway and halted in front of a small private house. Eduardo stopped short a hundred yards away. "Wait here," Lucy said. "I'll be back in a few minutes." She got out her camera, then climbed out and headed on foot toward the house, staying close to the edge of the undergrowth. Soon she approached the house. Lights had come on, and there were no curtains on the windows. She found a rock and threw it in the general area to check for dogs. None barked, so she moved closer and circled toward the back. Soon she was close enough to carefully push a branch aside and peer in a back window. She lifted her camera, looked through the viewfinder and positioned the camera, then began to fire away.

She watched from the edge of the window. Nathaniel stood to one side of the room with a beer in hand and watched the same thing she watched: a transaction being done. The two Americans stood by a wooden table in their pale suits, handing over stacks of cash. The young Mexican man across the table in turn handed over several artifacts. While the Americans examined the artifacts, the Mexican counted the money, then counted it again, stopping to wave a stack of bills toward Nathaniel, who came over to get it. Nathaniel then peeled money off his stack and handed it back to the short, pudgy American, Lewis Mon. Nathaniel pocketed the rest of his cut, and finished his beer while the two Americans carefully wrapped the artifacts in fabric, then placed them in cloth bags and set them on the table. Then Mon, the pudgy American, as if just remembering something, pulled out the money Nathaniel had returned to him, and counted it. When he finished, he grinned, saying something, and held out his hand to Nathaniel. A conversation ensued, the level of irritation visibly growing. Jack Partridge suddenly grabbed Nathaniel by the collar and shoved him against the wall. Up close he said nasty words. As he was snarling at him, Nathaniel happened to look out the window—and locked eyes with Lucy, who ducked quickly, but not quickly enough. She had been seen. Did she dare run? No. She waited, then chanced another look. Saw Partridge slap Nate hard across the face once, twice, three times. Saw Nate hand over his stack of bills. Partridge, utterly contemptuous, peeled a couple of hundreds off the stack and shoved them in Nate's T-shirt pocket. Lucy ran for her cab, clutching the camera that had recorded the whole sorry spectacle.

She had Eduardo hurry her back to town. Her friends had checked her into the hotel. She quickly found her room and locked herself in. She removed the memory chip, then hid it under the mattress and put another one in the camera. She stashed the camera behind a pillow in the back of the closet, and prepared to wait for Nathaniel.

After a while she got restless, struggling to stay awake, and decided on a more direct approach. She put on a clean shirt and went to Room seventeen and tried the skeleton key from her own room; enhanced with a bobby pin, it opened in a moment. The bedside lamp was left on. She locked herself in and had a look around. Clothes were strewn about, as were cigarette butt-filled ashtrays and empty bottles. A pair of tenor saxophones rested in a chair, carefully placed. She threw some clothes aside and sat on the bed, contemplating his chaos. He showed up half an hour later.

"Hi, Nate," she said, as the door swung open and she caught, for an instant, the wreckage of his face with his grinning guard down. Then he threw it back up.

"Lucy. Why, Lucy Ripken," he said softly, smiling at her. His cheeks were bruised just slightly, not so you'd notice unless you'd seen him slapped, hard, by Jack Partridge. "How are you? Or maybe I should say, how did you get yourself into mah room, woman?"

"I have my ways, Nate," Lucy said. "My wily ways."

"Well, yes," Nate said. "I imagine y'all do." He came over and sat near her on the bed, all amorous intention. And pure presumption. "But what might a wily woman want, this time a night, with a sax man such as I?"

"The truth, Nate," Lucy said sharply. "No bullshit. I know where you've been tonight, and I saw what that 'friend' of yours Partridge did to you."

"What the hell are you talking about?" he barked. "So that was you. I thought I saw somebody out that window. You followed me. You little bitch." He was enraged. "How dare you?"

"Skip the anger, bud. You're wasting your time. This is my job. I'm doing research, so bag your attitude."

"Shit," he said, getting up and grabbing one of his horns. "Can't a man do business without this kind of bullshit?"

"The guy that slapped your face, man. Why aren't you pissed at him instead of me?"

"Partridge? Oh, I'm plenty pissed at him, Lucy, but I also owe his people seventy-five thousand dollars, see? So if he wants to push me around a little, I gotta keep grinning and take it. You wanna jump into this mess, go right ahead."

"Seventy-five thousand? How did you manage that?"

"Gambling. I got in deep, kept playin' to get out, sure my luck would turn, but baby, it didn't. So when I met a guy who knows where to get the Precolombian goods, I jumped into the business."

"That's what you were doing tonight?"

"That's right, honey. Second trip. First was a trial run, did it for Maggie. And tonight little Jackie saw fit to slap me around because I tried to keep more than my shitty leftover share. I'd like to blow those fuckers away, if you really want to know, but I ain't capable of it and I think they are, which gives them a serious advantage."

"Jesus," said Lucy. "It's beginning to make sense now. But why are they here with you, Nathaniel? Didn't you bring the last stuff over yourself for Maggie?"

"Yeah, but these guys promised me they'd give me a break on my debt if I'd stop middlemanning it and let them directly at the source. Smuggling shit over the border's a walk in the park for dudes like them."

"Doesn't sound like a very good deal to me."

"Yeah, well, you take what Lewis Mon offers, Lucy. And I just want to get these guys off my case. Christ, so now what do you want? What do you want to do now that you've stuck your face into my business?"

"Hey, relax, man, I'm not going to—"

"What, turn me in? No, I guess not, not with all the 'evidence' you've amassed. Turn me in to who, anyway? My sister? Jesus, Lucy, why don't you just butt out. Shut up and butt out and let me finish paying my dues to these guys."

"Sure, Nate, sure. Just keep hauling the precious historical art of Mexico out of the country so it can sit in living rooms on Park Avenue. Don't you see the wrong in what you're doing?"

"Fuck no," he said. "It's just clay, for God's sake. Clay and stone. Sits in a room here, sits in a room there, what's the difference?"

Good question. "So what about the fakes?"

"Fakes? What fakes?"

"The ones in New York."

"I don't know anything about any fakes, Lucy. Stuff I took to Maggie was the real thing." He looked at her. "So now what?"

"So I'm going to bed. We'll try to figure it out tomorrow." She left Nathaniel, his cool forever lost, and went back to her room. To think she'd seen herself in bed with him. But, like he said, now what?

Upon opening the door, she discovered her room had been searched. She didn't have much in there, so things weren't all that torn up. They'd taken just two items: the camera from the closet, and the telegram from the pocket of her shirt. They missed the chip under the mattress.

5

In the Swim

Upon awakening, Lucy was bewildered for an instant. What neat, anonymous room was this? Then her eyes fell on her suitcase, waiting like a dog by the door, and she remembered. She had cleaned up last night, after discovering she'd been robbed of a camera and a telegram.

On first discovering the crime, displaying the baser instincts of an idiot female, she'd rushed to Nathaniel's room, seeking protection in the shadow of the nearest man she knew. What a blunder! Half-naked, he grudgingly accompanied her back to her room. Crashing hard in a late-night comedown, Nate had a complaint for a face, a flabby stomach, a farmer's tan, and foul breath from booze and cigarettes. Absorbed by his own troubles, he had nothing to offer—no sympathy, no explanation, not even a flicker of interest in what had happened in her room. He acted as if it had nothing to do with him.

Now came another day. She got out of bed, and watched the pale drapes warm with early light while she dressed. A knock came as she put on her shoes. She unlocked the door. Rosa was there. "Come in. Hey Rosita, how are you?"

"He's gone."

"Who's gone?"

"Nathaniel. Maggie went to wake him up, and found the room empty. At six a.m. What a weasel!"

"Gone? What the hell!" Lucy said. "Where's Maggie? You won't believe what happened last night. Damn, to think I thought that guy was so cool."

"Hey, he looked good from afar," said Rosa. "He had me fooled."

Upon hearing Lucy's story, Maggie said, "Well, now you know why I haven't seen much of Nate these last few years. He's gotten—"

"Rotten," said Lucy, interrupting. She felt angry and judgmental. "Corrupted by his own bad habits."

"Yes. I guess so," Maggie said, sadly. "From irresponsible to thoughtless to corrupt. My brother, the king of bad karma."

"But he's a hell of a musician," Lucy added. "That counts for something."

Lucy packaged the camera chip in a mailer and addressed it to Harold Ipswich in New York. She left it, and twenty dollars, with the desk clerk, who promised it would go out that day.

They were back at the ferry by noon, and reached South of Carolina around two o'clock in the somnolent heat of the afternoon. Neither Nathaniel nor Starfish had been around, according to the staff. The house was completely put together, and looked wonderful, fresh and light and airy. Even the pool had been emptied and cleansed of slime, and a man was busily repairing the cracked tiles. One of the workers had gotten the skiff cleaned up and its motor working, so they decided to visit Maggie's secret reef that afternoon to do some snorkeling, and forget about Precolombiana for a few hours.

They motored straight out from the beach in front of the house around three o'clock in the afternoon. Low tide was due close to four, and the reef lay about twenty minutes to the southeast. They would reach their destination, anchor, and orient themselves, then get into the water as the tide bottomed out and the coral came close to the surface, providing ideal conditions for free diving.

As they putted along, surging over the wind swells, Maggie ran the boat and talked about the reef. She had named it La Mancha because at the age of fourteen she had been reading Don Quixote when she discovered it one day on a boat trip with her mother. She didn't think anybody except the locals knew of its existence. None of the charter dive operations from Cancún or Isla ever brought people there. At least not in the old days. La Mancha lay so close to the surface that it occasionally emerged at minus tides.

For fifteen minutes or so they cruised southeast across a mile-wide, deep-water channel through which a slow southerly current pushed. Then the deep blue lightened up, the bottom rising to meet them. Through the clear jade water Lucy could see sand and rocks and coral below. On

Maggie's command Rosa threw the anchor over, and a few seconds later it caught. Maggie turned off the motor. They sat quietly in the gentle roll of the surf, protected from the larger swells by the reef.

They re-greased with sunscreen, then put on fins, masks, and snorkels. Maggie described the reef: "It stretches a couple hundred yards north to south and fifty yards or so across. You can float along this side, and the current through here will carry you south. When you get to the end—it drops off pretty abruptly—swim back on the other side. Be careful over the middle, there's a couple of shallow spots, and the coral is sharp."

Over the side she flopped. Rosa followed. Lucy gave a last tug on the anchor chain, then went overboard into the warm, clear water.

She swam side-by-side with Rosa, floating along behind Maggie, parallel to the edge of the reef. They drifted on the surface in twenty or thirty feet of water. Purple sea fans waved in slow motion on the bottom, amidst enormous clumps of brain coral. Large fish darted from cave to cave amongst the rocks, and hundreds of smaller fish swirled in rainbow-hued schools. Lucy lifted the lower rim of her mask to let a little water in, then swished it around to clear the glass. The current carried them slowly along. On the right, the sandy bottom dropped away into deeper water, with schools of big fish darting, glinting in the eerie blue-gold half-light. Brilliantly colored fish and plants and coral reeled past in a slow underwater ballet, a luminous and thrilling dance. Lucy, hearing nothing but the sound of her own breathing, fell into a trance, hypnotized by the interplay of color, motion, and light.

Maggie swerved left, pumping harder with her fins over a shallow stretch of reef. Lucy and Rosa followed, skimming coral that appeared to thrust close to the surface. Glittering fish scattered before them. After a moment they slowed and found a footing on a smooth rock ledge. The water was thigh deep. Perched like ungainly birds on their flippered feet, they pushed up their masks and spit out their snorkels. "Incredible," said Rosa. "Did you see all the angel fish?"

"I can never remember their names," said Lucy, "but there were so many. The colors are amazing."

"Psychedelic," said Maggie. "Especially the parrot fish. Isn't this great?" she exclaimed, taking in the vast blue surroundings. "We are standing up in the middle of the ocean! Damn," she added, squinting into the distance to the north. "Here comes a boat. What a rude racket!" They watched as a fast-moving speedboat approached, banging aggressively over the swells, engine roaring. Their own little boat was two hundred yards away, at the other end of the reef. "I guess La Mancha is a secret no longer."

"Oh well," said Lucy. "It has been ten years, Mags. Everything changes."

"Hey, what are those people doing?" Rosa said. The speedboat—one of those cigarette models that look like big streamlined dicks, make a lot of noise, and go nine million miles an hour—had pulled up close to the skiff. A man jumped from the cigarette into the skiff, and quickly tossed a line back. Then he untied the smaller boat's anchor line and threw it overboard. He jumped back into the cigarette boat, and after a moment it started moving again toward them. Tied on, the skiff bounced along behind it.

"What the hell," said Maggie. "Hey," she yelled, waving her arms. "Hey, down here." They all shouted and waved. "Well, they're coming our way," Maggie said. "But why'd they cut my anchor loose?"

"Damn," said Lucy. She was the first to recognize them, because she'd seen a lot more of them. Jack Partridge and Lewis Mon. "I think we got trouble, girls."

The boat roared up, stopping thirty yards away in deeper water. "Everything all right, ladies?" Mon called out pleasantly. "Having a good dive?"

"That's my boat," said Maggie. "What do you think you're doing with—"

"Hi, ladies," said the black-haired woman who'd been seated with her back to Lucy at Mon's and Partridge's table last night, now popping into view on the deck. She abruptly threw off her black wig, took off her shades, and shook out her long blond hair. Starfish, in a bikini bottom and nothing else. "How're the fishies? Are they biting?" She smiled, her teeth gleaming.

"Starfish!!"

"That's right, baby. The one and only." She slipped her shades back on and put an arm around Jack Partridge. "Now, just so you know what's going on, Margaret. Lucy Ripken here was following your dear brother Nathaniel, and Jack and Lewis last night, when they had some business to transact over there in Tikiville. She took some pictures she really shouldn't have taken. But the smart little lady didn't know that I followed her; and I tried to get the film, only she was so clever she had already taken it out of the camera. So if you'll be so kind as to let us know where that film is, Lucy Ripken, we'll leave your boat and be off to fetch it."

Rosa and Maggie looked at her. Lucy said, "I don't know what you're talking about." Damn, she didn't have a clue. What to say? Where was Harry when she needed him? How had she missed Starfish at the Villa Maya? Truth or not? She blurted out, "It's in the house. I gave it to—"

"Uh uh," said Lewis. "No good. We already looked around. And checked with the staff."

"I sent it to New York. It wasn't film, it's a digital camera and I sent the memory chip with the images to a friend. With instructions not to do anything without hearing from me."

"That was a bad idea," said Starfish. She talked baby-talk when she talked tough. "A very bad idea."

"Well, tide's out. You enjoy your dive now, ladies," Lewis added, revving up the engine of the cigarette.

"Wait a minute," Maggie said. "You can't just drive off and leave us. The tide's going to come up and—"

"Your little yacht here will be found capsized somewhere, oh, not too far away," said Jack Partridge. "All that's left after a very unfortunate boating accident."

"Unfortunate indeed," added Lewis Mon.

"Nathaniel is going to be sooo upset," Starfish cooed. "I'll have to take care of him."

"You're not going to get away with this," Lucy said bravely. "There's no way." So now she knew what the bad guys do. Kill people who threaten their interests; and do it rather blithely.

Lewis Mon wheeled the cigarette boat around to the north. "Here's lunch," Jack Partridge laughed, emptying a plastic bucket of chum—bloody fishguts and heads—overboard as Mon accelerated and they zoomed away, the little skiff bouncing along behind. The three women watched their Panama hats blow out of the skiff. The speedboat veered off to the northeast. Stunned at the abrupt turn of events, they stared until it disappeared. It didn't take long.

"Shark bait," Maggie said. "What the hell."

"Oh my God," Rosa wailed, fighting back tears. "Now what are we going to do?"

"Stay right here for now," Maggie said. "It's too shallow for sharks. By the time the tide comes in the chum'll be gone, and we can—" She left the sentence unfinished. They stood on a little reef in thirty inches of water, a mile offshore, with a deepwater channel separating them from land. Inevitably, the tide would rise.

"We can what?" Rosa cried. "What are we gonna do? Jesus, Lucy, why did you have to go sneaking around?"

"I'm sorry, Rosa. I was just doing my job," Lucy said. "I had no idea—damn, look at that!" A shark fin surfaced about fifty yards away, headed straight for the chum, and a second joined it. The fins reached their goal, the water boiled, then stillness returned.

"Oh my God," moaned Rosa. "What if they're coming this way?"

"Don't worry," said Maggie. "They won't come up on the reef. It's too shallow. At least we can be thankful for that."

"I'm going to swim to the island," Lucy announced.

"Swim?! Get serious, Lucy," said Maggie. "It's over a mile away."

"The tide's going to rise in a couple of hours, and then what? I don't think Lloyd Bridges is in the neighborhood, Maggie," Lucy said. "I swim nearly a mile in the pool almost every day back in the city. I can do it. You guys wait here, I'll get a boat and come back for you."

"If the sharks don't get you," Rosa said.

"They won't bother me before nightfall. That's when they normally feed," Lucy said. "Once all that crud dissipates they'll be gone."

"Yeah, hope so," Maggie said. "Well, the current moves that way," she added, nodding south. "So you'll have to point up there." She indicated the north end of the island.

"Right. I'll use the fins but not the snorkel and mask. Too bulky."

"Hey, Lucy," said Maggie. "I'd go, but—"

"I'm a strong swimmer," Lucy said. "It doesn't make sense for two of us to do it."

"Right," said Maggie.

She handed Rosa her mask, then hugged her. "If there was a horse to ride you'd be going, Rosie. But I'm the swimmer here. Well, no time to waste, I guess." She gave Maggie a quick hug.

"There's a lighthouse at the south end of the island, just under the point," said Maggie. "With the current that's probably where you'll end up. You'll see a Mayan ruin up on the cliff, and the lighthouse is right below it. Over there." She pointed down the island. They were too far off to make out any details.

"Well, wish me luck, girls," Lucy said. They did. Then she pushed off quickly and began her swim. She skimmed over the shallows to the east side of the reef, and headed north, swimming slowly and steadily, just as if she was doing her hundred laps in the pool. That was five thousand feet, close to a mile, and she swam it every day. Chlorine and obnoxious lane hogs, however, made for less adversarial freestyling than did ocean currents and sharks. At the top of the reef she turned more westerly, on a tack that would take her to the northern tip of Isla Mujeres, if there were no currents to contend with.

Lucy launched into the deep waters, feeling small and vulnerable but certain that she could make it. She had never swum long distance in a fight with a current, and didn't intend to here. Instead, she would point north and let it push her along, half-riding and half-resisting, and hit the island at the south end. As she found a steady rhythm she let her breathing take over, and with every exhalation pushed out the images that rushed her, at first—images of herself on the surface, seen from below, from the shark's point of view. From there, she looked like a lively little snack. She forced the images away, counting her strokes, telling herself not to check her progress until she'd reached a thousand. Once she'd gotten well clear of the reef the swells grew larger, and she rose up and drifted down with them, occasionally finding her shoulder buried deep, making the stroke harder, or flailing the air as she broke free of the water.

At a thousand strokes she stopped. The abrupt halt disoriented her, and she thrashed, briefly panicked. A wave hit her in the face and filled her mouth with salt water. Choking it out, she surfaced with a lunge, gasped "Oh, shit," and then internalized her voice: be calm, be calm, breathe slowly, slowly and deeply. She regained her composure. Treading water and controlling her breath, she surveyed the scene. She felt tiny beneath the huge blue sky, surrounded by dark blue water. Looking back, she couldn't see over the waves to where her friends waited on the reef. Ahead, the island loomed, although it didn't look any closer than before. And she felt tired. The water pushed at her, pushed and pushed. She was moving south at a faster pace than she had anticipated. She would have to swim harder, or miss the island completely. Cancún was the next stop, ten miles southwest. She would never make it that far, even if the current chose to push her that way and not southeast, out to sea just in time for dinner.

Lucy fought off the looming panic. Pointing more sharply north, she started up again at a slightly faster pace. This time she vowed not to look again until she'd done two thousand strokes.

At fifteen-hundred she stopped for another look. The island loomed larger now, but she had drifted further south. It would be close. A cramp hit the arch of her left foot. She grabbed, rubbed it out. Her shoulders ached. She drifted alone in the middle of the ocean, exhausted, frightened, responsible for three lives. The last time her life had been so threatened, a psychotic woman had pointed a gun at her. On a Jamaican beach. Harry Ipswich. She swam on, thinking about Harry, and how much she loved him. She would see him again, and let him know. Why wasn't he here to help her out? Because she had discouraged him. She had wanted to handle this story on her own. She was an independent woman.

And so she would die alone. The thought flashed through, she couldn't help it. Lucy swam on, crawling endlessly against her own exhaustion, eyes salt-stung, back burning from sun and salt, half-choking on salt water that slipped into her mouth and down her raw, tender throat. Her right shoulder ached. The cramp in her left foot returned. She swam through the pain, swam and swam and swam into a state of mind beyond weariness, beyond the evil baby voice of Isabel Starfish Chapin (Chapin—where else had she seen that name?), beyond anything she'd ever known, where the water was a tunnel she thrashed through forever; a sunsplashed vortex filled with rippling, roaring light; and then there were fins flashing and the sharks came and she knew she would die; except that they were dolphins, dancing on the whitecaps, circling her with their wise, friendly faces. They came close, watching her curiously as she labored. She was too tired to talk as she struggled on, but she tried to communicate with them telepathically. Wasn't that how they did it? Come here, Mr. Dolphin, come here and give me a lift to shore, I need a ride, baby, can't we glide together I promise I'll buy you all a beer and a fish dinner at the restaurant of your choice perhaps Le Bernardin? if you'll only give me a ride. They swam away, leaping over the waves that had begun to wash over her head. Lucy stopped. She looked. She was maybe halfway in, and almost all the way past the end of the island. Against the falling sun she could just make out the ruins above, the lighthouse below. She wouldn't make it.

Then she heard a motor, lunging erratically over the waves. She screamed, she thrashed, she kicked her feet hard with a last flurry of energy and managed to get high enough out of the water to spy a little boat headed north a hundred yards away. She flapped her arms with a shriek and fell back, exhausted. A moment later two Mexican fishermen dragged her out of the water into their boat. She didn't speak much Spanish and they didn't speak English, but she managed to make them understand about the *dos señoritas* on the rocks. They headed out across the channel.

Fifteen minutes later they found Maggie and Rosa, treading chest-deep water. Maggie had tied the ankle strap of her left fin to a knob on the reef with three rubber mask straps knotted together so they wouldn't drift away, and Rosa held her hand. As soon as the fishermen pulled Rosa and then Maggie aboard, the three women burst into hysterical tears, hugging so hard they almost capsized the little boat before the two fishermen could turn around and head back toward Isla Mujeres.

Lucy took stock as they bounced over the waves, headed home. A blister on her left heel, where the fin had rubbed it raw; sunburned shoulders; aches, pains, and exhaustion. Her friends were burned and weary. Not so bad, considering how close they had come. She had given up. If that boat hadn't appeared she would have gone down, her friends close behind.

The fishermen dropped them off on the beach in front of the house. Maggie had the men wait while she ran into the house and returned a moment later with a hundred-dollar bill. They refused it at first, then took it. They would probably spend weeks talking about the three biggest fish they ever caught, and the price they fetched.

As they putted away in their little boat, Rosa said, "God sent them." Apparently she'd gotten a dose of religion out there along with the sun and salt water. Lucy didn't feel like arguing the point. Someone had kept the sharks off her ass.

Maggie said, "Yeah, I guess. Meanwhile, Nate's in the house. He's drunk." On cue, the sound of the saxophone drifted out. Slow, slow blues. They looked that way. The sun had gone down behind the island.

They found him lying on his back on the long dining table, wearing bikini underwear and sunglasses, playing the mournful horn, with a bottle of gold tequila close by. A cigarette smoldered on the edge of the table, next to another one that had been set on the table and forgotten, burning a black scar onto it. "Hey, ladies," Nate muttered when they came in. "What's happenin'?" He honked his horn.

"Damn you, Nathaniel," said Maggie. "Get off the darn table."

"Hey, take it easy, sis," he slurred, swinging his feet off the table and sitting up. "Wow, you guys got a little too much sun today, huh?" He grinned. "Those rays can be fierce, eh?"

"Where's your ladyfriend Starfish?" Maggie snapped.

"Starfish? I don't know. Haven't seen her since—"

"She ran off with your 'friends' Jack and Lewis?"

He looked puzzled. "Yeah. I guess. Hey, what's the difference? Plenty of ladies here now, eh?" He stood, honked a riff, and grinned at Lucy. "What's cookin', Lucy in the Sky?"

She would have grabbed him by the collar and slammed him against the wall if he had a collar to grab. Instead, she said, "Nate, you're a stupid fuck, do you know that? A first-class, stupid fucking asshole!" she snarled, putting enough into it to actually get the idiot's attention for a moment.

"Hey, hey, take it easy, baby. Check this out." He put the horn to his lips and blew the opening lines from "Girl from Ipanema," sambaing down the room in his underwear.

"Mother of God!" Maggie shouted, shutting him up. "Your friends just tried to kill us, you son of a cur. I can't believe you. You're like a—you're jes' like you were when you were fifteen, only now you're thirty-three."

"What are you talking about?" he said.

"Starfish was there, too, Nate," Lucy said. He was watching them, but sweeping the table with his arm, searching for the tequila bottle. He found it and brought it toward his mouth. Maggie lunged at him and swatted it across the room. It shattered on the tile floor.

"They tried to kill us, Nathaniel," Maggie shrieked. "Your girlfriend and those evil men you brought down here from Dallas tried to drown us today, Natty! Can you hear me?"

"You didn't have to do that," he said. "Go breaking my bottle."

"Fuck it," said Rosa. "He's not going to hear you, Maggie. Forget it." She looked straight at him. "He's just a piece of human wreckage that washed up on the beach. If we're lucky he'll wash away again."

Maybe it was that Rosa had said so few words to him until that moment; or maybe it was her tone. Whatever the reason, her words seemed to penetrate the tequila fog in Nathaniel's brain. He stared at her, a stupid grin flickering and then dying on his face. "You have no right to talk to me like that," he said. "This is—I'm a—" He clutched his horn. The three women watched him. His eyes were cast down, shoulders slumped.

"I'll get some coffee made," Maggie said. "Come on, Nathaniel. Why don't you put some clothes on? We've got a lot to talk about."

After showering away some of the aches, pains, and sunburn, and changing into fresh clothes, they gathered around the long dining table, with coffee, fruit, bread, and cheese, as night fell over the sea beyond the patio and beach. The women told Nathaniel parts of what they knew, and finished where they had begun, with the attempted triple murder— what else could they call it?—at sea earlier the same day.

"But how could Starfish be involved with them?" he said. "I've known her for years. We've always looked out for each other."

"How did you meet those guys?" Lucy asked.

"I don't know. I mean, I had a bookie in Dallas and when my bill got out of control and time came to collect he sent them."

"Well, she arrived here with them, Nate," said Maggie. "They checked into the Boca together a couple days before you got here."

"But that's impossible!"

"No, it's the truth," said Lucy. "What's impossible is for me to believe you didn't recognize her the other night at the Villa Maya. You knew she was there—so you had to know she was the one who broke into my room. You knew she was working with them, Nate. Why are you lying? Why are you protecting her? She tried to kill your sister, for God's sake!"

"I don't know," he said, faltering. "We have this little game we play, where she dresses up, wears that wig and pretends she's someone else, and then—but she didn't know them before. She would have—"

"Who was she playing the game for, Nate? You? Or was it Partridge?"

"She plays for whoever pays, I guess."

"Pays? What is she, some kind of hooker?" Maggie snapped. "Is that your lady love's true calling?"

"No, no, it's nothing that cut and dried, Mags," he said. "She—just—Fuck, I don't know. She does what she has to." Funny thing, Lucy thought. Starfish had said the same thing about him.

He took a deep breath, taking stock, and fixed his gaze on Lucy. "You want your Precolombian art story? You wanna know how it works? What the fuck, I'll tell you," he said. "Here's the deal. I met this guy down here last year. He works for this artist named Alberto Gutierrez who is really famous for making perfect copies of Precolombian pieces."

"Yes, I know who he is. But what's your guy's name?" Lucy asked. She was taking notes.

"It doesn't matter. So anyways—"

"Yes it does," she interrupted.

"Okay, okay. His name's Tomas. Just Tomas. So Tomas knows another guy who works in this little private museum in Merida—a museum endowed by a local gringo dope millionaire who happens to have an incredible collection of Mayan stuff and doesn't know shit about it. He just buys it because it's expensive, know what I mean? So me and Tomas—Tomas figured it out, I'm just his ticket across the border—came up with a way to make a lot of money. It's very simple, really. Gutierrez marks his copies with a secret code that can only be read by an infrared sensor, but you know who actually applies those code markings? Tomas. So this is how it works.

"First, Tomas takes a Gutierrez copy of one of the pieces in the dope guy's museum, and they are damned good copies, aged to perfection. And he doesn't mark it with the ID mark. Instead, he gets his friend—he gets a cut too, of course—to switch the copy with the original, so there's no theft reported. Then he codes the original, so everybody in on the scam assumes it's a copy, and I take it over the border in a batch of Gutierrez copies, some coded and others uncoded. They get all mixed together, and only I know which ones are 'real' and which ones are fake. Then I go to my friend Hamilton Walking Wind—went to school with Ham—and his amigo Calvin Hobart, who provide me with the documents I need, which describe the uncoded fakes as real, giving them legitimate history so I can sell them for good money. Meanwhile, the real pieces ended up in your hot little hands, Mags."

They sat quietly for a moment, thinking it over. Lucy broke the silence. "So you're smuggling fakes that are real, and real pieces that are fakes."

"And just plain fakes, too. Pretty cool, huh?"

"Sure, Nathaniel," said Maggie. "Except that your friends left us to die out there today, and your other friends in New Mexico—Hamilton Walking Wind and Calvin Hobart—are already dead."

He looked shocked. "Dead? Hamilton? What?"

Maggie said, "Can't you grasp the implications of what you've done? You let me sell fake goods to those people in New York, and got Rosa's boyfriend involved, and now we're all in this unholy mess."

"What happened to Cal and Ham?"

"The cops are calling it double suicide," said Lucy. "Because they were HIV positive."

"No way," he said. "The whole point of this deal for them was to get more money they needed for special treatments for the virus. That's why they were willing to cook up those bogus documents. There's no way they would have done it otherwise. Fuck. Hamilton dead. Really, Mags, I had no idea somebody else was going to double-check authenticity in New York. Honest."

"You blithering idiot, Nathaniel," Maggie said.

"But what about the pieces those guys just paid cash for? Who's going to cook the documents on those?" asked Lucy.

"The papers were done in advance. Starfish brought them down. But Mon and Partridge think they're authentic. That's why they paid all that money for them the other night."

"So Starfish knew Hamilton and Hobart, too?" Lucy said. "God, quadruple cross."

"Yeah. I introduced them. Sure. Everybody passes through Santa Fe one time or another. It's, you know, Precolombian central. Right now Starfish is with Partridge, but she knows the pieces are fake and Jack and Lewis don't. I cut a deal with her."

"I would bet Jack Partridge and Lewis Mon passed through Santa Fe, too," Lucy said grimly. "Very recently."

"You don't think they did Calvin and Hamilton?"

"Of course they did. My guess is that Hobart and Walking Wind got cold feet about continuing to authenticate fakes—or maybe got word from New York about what had happened in the gallery—and they were going to own up to forging the papers. They paid the price for trying to reclaim their ethics, I guess."

"My God," said Rosa after a pause. "What a mess of lies and deception."

"But why did they—Nathaniel, I never . . . nothing I ever said to you suggested any of these pieces were worth murdering anybody. Now there are two people dead and they almost killed us, too," Maggie said, still shocked at Nathaniel's behavior. "They just left us out there, Nate. Left us with the sharks and blood in the water. They wanted us dead! And she was with them! How can you trust her?"

"I bet she was planning to come back for you," he said lamely.

"Christ, Nate, don't be a fool," said Lucy. "Sure, she might have come back—to watch the sharks feed. No way she had anything else in mind. So tell me again about the two pieces from the other night?"

"They're each one of a kind. If they were real, with good papers, probably half a mil apiece. Mon paid fifty thousand dollars for them, and he's sure he's making a killing. Only he doesn't know they're fake."

"When he finds out he'll kill you, too," said Maggie.

"Not gonna happen, sis," he said. "There's a buyer in Dallas already set up. They'll go right into a private collection and that's that. Soon as Mon collects the money I'm out of debt, and Partridge and Mon are now Tomas's problem—but he doesn't know that. I've just gotta hook up with Starfish to get my share when she gets her cut at the other end. Then I'm outta this deal for good. And this country. I'm going to Raratonga soon as I get what's mine."

"How much is that?" Lucy asked quietly.

"They're supposed to pay her a hundred thousand once the deal is done. Our deal was she'd cut me half but I'm sure she'll cry poor. Probably give me thirty or forty grand. That should get me goin' again."

"Mother of God, Nathaniel, I can't believe it. You've left a trail of death and destruction across two countries," said Maggie.

"Hey, let's not get so self-righteous, sis," he said. "Don't forget you're the one who said you'd be willing to pay just about anything for the two pieces I got you."

"Oh, nonsense, Nathaniel," Maggie said fiercely. "How dare you! You know I would never want anybody dead for an artifact."

"Yeah, well, I didn't exactly plan on it either," he said sullenly.

"You didn't plan on much, did you?" Maggie snapped.

"That's enough, Maggie," said Lucy. "Beating up on him now isn't gonna solve anything."

"That may be easy for you to say, Lucy. You've got your story. But I've got some dead friends in Santa Fe, and my little brother helped kill them."

"Shut the fuck up, Maggie," Nathaniel snarled. "I didn't kill anybody, goddammit."

"Hey, hey," said Rosa. "This fingerpointing is stupid. He's right, Maggie. He didn't kill those boys. I can understand why you're angry, but what's the point? We've got enough problems without you two shouting at each other. Like what are we going to do?" She looked at Lucy. "Hey Luce, the question is, what now? What next? You think you have enough info for your story, or perhaps you would rather mess with Jack and Lewis again? I personally would prefer to get my sunburnt buns back to Santa Fe and get on my horse and ride about nine million miles into the desert and hide out for a few weeks on solid ground. No waves, no water, and no bloody Precolombian art." She burst into tears. "Jesus Christ, we were dead out there today, Lucy! Dead!" Lucy went to her, and put an arm around her.

"I know, Rosa, I know. If I hadn't seen those guys in the boat—I was going down when I heard them." After a moment, as Rosa calmed down, Lucy glanced over at Nathaniel. He was looking at the table. "So where is the little woman, Nate?"

He met her gaze. "Starfish? She's supposed to show up here tonight."

They heard the Harley from quite a distance, and calmly moved out onto the patio, where the three of them sat in darkness facing the black sky and sea. Nate stayed in the living room to greet her, play the game out, see where it took them.

Inside, he picked up the horn and played a soft jazzy riff as Starfish came in the front door at the other end of the house. "Nate?" she called urgently, all sweet concern. "Baby, you here?"

"Back here, babe," he said. They heard it all, sitting on the patio in silence.

"Nate, my God, when I heard—I was down at Kentucky Fried when I heard they found the skiff." She rushed into the room sounding breathless. "Your boat capsized out there. Baby, did you hear? Did you hear what happened to-day? Nate, Margaret and her friends were out there, and—"

"And I swam in," Lucy said, filing into the room, followed by Margaret and Rosa. Starfish was wearing skintight black leather pants with fringe down the sides, and a black leather jacket unzipped, with a black bra. She looked like the perfect embodiment of violent sex, nasty and dangerous.

"Omigod," Starfish shrieked. She went white under her tan for an instant, but didn't miss a beat. "I'm so glad to see you. I was going to come back for you out there today but I couldn't get away from Jack and Louie, those guys are so crazy but I had to pretend that I was into it, too, you know, so that they wouldn't—I was planning to go get another boat but Jackie, he—"

"Please be quiet," Maggie said calmly. "There's nothing, not a single thing you can say, Starfish, that will change what happened out there today. You know that."

"But I was coming back. Honest I was." She looked at Nate. "Nate, you don't really think that I would be party to—"

"Sure, babe," he said wearily. "Whatever you say."

"Isabel Chapin," said Lucy. "I probably should have had my DEA friend check on you when he checked out Partridge and Mon. Maybe then I wouldn't have missed you in the bar the other night."

"DEA, huh." Starfish was beginning to see how this was going to play out. She looked at Nathaniel, and got tough. "Nate, I've gotta get my things. I'm going back to Texas tonight. They're waiting. Call me in a couple of days."

"They know, babe," he said.

"Know what?" she said.

"About the deal. The Texas deal."

"What? You told them? You stupid fuck, Nathaniel," she snarled, then turned on Lucy. "There's nothing you can do. Nate doesn't know who the buyer is, so if you mess this up, you'll wish you had gone down out there, ladies. You understand?"

"Hey, back off, bitch," said Lucy. This woman pissed her off. "We don't have any interest in screwing up your ugly little deal. But let me tell you this, Star-fucking-fish. I'm going to nail you, and your friends, one way or another. You understand, sweetheart?"

Starfish just smiled at her. "I'm going to get my things. Been nice meeting you all. Nate," she tuned in on him, and her voice sharpened.

"Yeah, babe."

"Call me in Dallas. And don't mess this up, darling."

"Fuck you," Rosa shrieked as Starfish strode across the room. "Fuck you wherever you live and forever," she shouted fiercely as the black leather–clad bitch headed upstairs. "God, do we have to just let her go?" Rosa asked.

"What else can we do?" Lucy said.

"I don't know," Rosa said. "Maybe rip her tits off and feed them to the sharks?"

"I don't think they'd be edible," said Margaret. "Otherwise I'd say go for it."

The three of them checked out Nate. He looked like a traumatized rubber man, spineless, collapsing in on himself.

"You sure know how to pick 'em, Nate," said Margaret.

Starfish roared off an hour later without further words with any of them. They had talked of detaining her, or—only half-jokingly—shooting her dead, but decided against it. Instead, Maggie posted workers with machetes at the gate, on the beach, and around the house.

Rosa left the next morning. She'd had enough. She missed her man, her horse, her dogs, and the desert. Nathaniel was to leave later that day, while Maggie had agreed to stick around with Lucy for another day or two of research in Ticul. They were going to try to find Alberto Gutierrez, his man Tomas, and the private museum in Merida Nathaniel had described.

Before he left, Nathaniel said just one thing to Lucy. "You can do what you want with what I've told you, Lucy, but if you publish my name in your article I'm a dead man."

"Even in Raratonga?"

"Even in Raratonga."

They couldn't find Tomas, who hadn't been seen around the studio for a couple of days. The house where Lucy had seen the deal done was empty. Gutierrez was off "somewhere in Oaxaca," an assistant said, visiting a silver mine. Nor did anybody at the studio know anything about a private museum in Merida. They had a good look at some of Gutierrez's amazingly authentic forgeries, but otherwise, the trip produced nothing. And so, after one day on the road and a last quiet day under a palm tree on the beach, Lucy and Maggie headed back to Santa Fe.

6

Lucy in Love

Lucy, on a red-eye east out of Albuquerque, stared out into the frozen blackness and contemplated the complex after-taste of Santa Fe. After eleven hours of fly-then-wait through Merida, Guadalajara, Dallas, and Albuquerque, she and Maggie had arrived at the Santa Fe Airport close to midnight two days back. Jedediah Crowtooth met them in the truck.

Back at Maggie's house on the mountaintop, a string of messages from Rosa awaited her, conveying with some ur-gency that Quentin Washington had called repeatedly. Lucy called Rosa, and woke Darren. "Yeah?" he muttered.

"Um, hi, Darren, it's Lucy."

"It's late, Lucy. She's asleep. Can't it wait till tomor-row?" He was rather snappish.

"You tell me, Darren. I was calling because my friend Quentin's been calling Rosa the last two days and she left a message up here at Maggie Clements's house that it was important. Several messages, I should say."

"Oh." He paused. "Sorry. Just a minute." He dropped the phone on the bed. "Rosey. Hey, Rosa, wake up. It's Lucy. I guess they're back."

Lucy waited. After a few seconds Rosa came on. "Hey, Luce, sorry, we went to bed early. I was riding all day."

"Fine, sorry I woke you, but tell the boy he needn't be so gruff. You only left six anxious messages up here, Toots."

"I know, I know. He's not good late at night. Anyways, yeah, your friend Quentin kept calling. He sounded freaked."

"Did he say what was up?"

"I asked but he said it was confidential."

"Okay. Well, I should call him." She paused. "Um, so how are you doing?"

"Not bad. Felt great to be back in the saddle."

"I bet. No rising tides in the desert, eh?" She paused. "You and Darren doing all right?"

"What do you mean? Yeah, we're fine. Why?"

"I was just a little worried. I mean, he didn't really want you to go, remember?"

"Right. Well . . . " She hesitated. "I guess in a way he was right, wasn't he?"

"What do you mean?"

"What do I mean? What do you think, Luce? We almost died down there. If I hadn't been there it wouldn't have happened."

"Hmm. Yes, I suppose that's one way of looking at it," Lucy said. "Hey, I'm going back to New York day after tomorrow. So let's get together for lunch, eh?"

"Aren't you going to stay with us tomorrow night?"

"Maggie says I can stay up here. She's got a ton of room, and Claud's really happy here."

"That's right. You've joined Dog Nation. But I really wanted to prove to you that I finally learned how to cook. Kind of, that is. I do killer fish tacos anyways. You want to come for lunch *mañana*?"

"You don't need to cook for me, Rosie. I know it's not your strong suit."

"Hey, watch it, Luce." She laughed. "But you know what? You're right, and you talked me out of it. Let's hook up at the Badger Bistro instead. One okay? I want to put in some studio time in the morning."

"Sounds good. See you then."

"It's across the square from the Anasazi. You can't miss the giant blue badger holding a wine glass on the sign."

Next she'd called Quentin Washington in New York, who launched into a tirade even though it was three o'clock in the morning back there. "Lucy, is that you? Finally! Jesus, these motherfuckers threatened my wife. My wife and child, for God's sake! What the hell is going on, and how the hell did I get involved?! My God, Lucy, I have a family, for crying out loud. How dare you—"

"Hey, hey, wait a minute, Quentin." Lucy finally got in a word. "Now tell me what's up?"

He calmed a little. "I got this call. Some guy, won't say his name, says if I don't authenticate those damn fakes or at least keep my mouth shut about it I'm in deep shit, like, he goes into this creepy singsong voice, 'You know your old friend Calvin Hobart,' Quentin, and I said sure, and he said, 'Well, you know what happened to him, don't you?'

Hell, the way he was talking I figured I'd better play along so I said sure, and he went, 'Well, how are the apartments at 716 W. 199th St.? Are they spacious and nice?' and then, 'How's young Hannah doing these days? And your pregnant wife, Beth, how is she?' Jesus, Lucy, he knew everything about me. So he gets off the phone and after several sleepless hours I called around to find out. Christ, why didn't you tell me what had happened to Calvin? He and his partner are dead, for God's sake!"

"I know, I know, I was going to tell you but I never got a chance to call. I met the bad boys that did it, I think, down in Ticul."

"So you saw Gutierrez? What do you think of his operation? Is there a connection? Are those guys the same ones that called me? I phoned Rooney to tell her to call her goons off and she claimed she had no idea what I was talking about. She does do outrage convincingly, doesn't she? What a snake! Jesus, I don't know who's behind these dudes if it isn't her, but they sure sound nasty."

"They are more than that, bub. I'll tell you about it in a day or two when I get back. I don't know if it's the same guys, to tell the truth. Of course Rooney's playing dumb, what else could she possibly do? Threaten you herself? That ninety-pound nightmare? Fat chance. What's the latest on the fakes?"

"Last I heard, Forte's going to do her bidding."

"So what do they want from you?"

"Like I said, basically they want me to keep my mouth shut."

"You have a problem with that?"

"Well, not exactly, except that I already told a couple of people at work about the scene at the gallery the other day, so it's a little late for secrecy. And the Precolombian art world is pretty ingrown."

"Yeah, well, it may be ingrown but from what I've seen, it's plenty nasty too, man."

"You just came in on the wrong end of a deal."

"No shit, Quentin. So what are you going to do?"

"Man, I don't know. These guys know my family, they know my address, they even know I got popped for selling hashish in Austin in 1975. I mean, it was a set-up, I had, like, six grams and they called me a major distributor, but it's still on the record. I had to cop a plea to get out of jail."

"They knew that?"

"They're fucking with me, Lucy. Threatening a scandal to ruin my career. In this bullshit time we live in, it could happen. And I could even handle it, but the way they talk about Hannah and Beth just scares my ass. If I lose my shot at the Vermont gig because of this, well, Christ, I don't know what I'm going to do."

"No shit." Lucy pictured Partridge and Mon, grinning as they sped away in their cigarette boat. But how could they know about Quentin? She hadn't explored the possibility of a link between that end of the deal and this. Quentin's phone call certainly raised the issue. But maybe the link didn't exist. Maybe Madeleine Rooney *had* hired someone to harass him. She seemed capable of it. "Was it just one guy on the call?"

"Yeah. He was talking like this." He lapsed into a hoarse whisper. "So between that and the singsong I couldn't really get a fix on his voice."

"Well, we'll sort it out, like I said. See you in a couple days."

"Right, Luce. And keep me posted, for God's sake. There's some heavy shit going down here, and I don't want it landing on my family."

When Lucy called to confirm lunch in the morning, Darren, speaking for Rosa, who was out on her horse, said she wouldn't be able to make it because his parents were coming to town on short notice and they had to drive to Albuquerque to pick them up. And so Lucy and Rosa didn't get a chance to see each other again, or even to say good-bye. Lucy felt that as a little void in her heart. For some reason she hadn't quite nailed down, she was deeply worried about Rosa.

On the flight home, she dozed off, dreaming of female shadows tumbling in graceful slow motion through the depthless water, and woke with a start as the descent into LaGuardia was announced. She fished out her makeup bag and freshened lipstick and eyeshadow, brushed her hair, and studied herself in the mirror.

At LaGuardia, after the interminable taxi to the gate and hold, Lucy wearily rose with the late night stragglers and filed off the plane and into the antic flow of New York, dragging her camera bags. She wore an elegant new western-style black silk shirt Maggie had given her, along with black jeans and the jean jacket Harold had given her. Dressed in gifts, she was alone, exhausted, and depressed. There would be no one there to meet her. There never was. At least Señor Claud would be with her, eager to get out of his traveling cage and home to his life in loftland. Her new true blue love, Claud the Poodle.

Through the gauntlet of limo hustlers and into baggage claim to pick up a bag from the carousel and a dog from the special claims area Lucy trudged, dragging her two camera bags all the while. She found her bag, then found the counter behind which waited the poodle in a cage. A moment later, on a brand-new leash Maggie had given her, she had the dog too, and she headed out, bent under the load of luggage, dragging a cowering, half-stoned dog who'd never lived anywhere but the wild high desert and now wandered through LaGuardia Airport leashed to a woman he hardly knew.

Lucy stepped out into cold spring air and airport racket, preparing herself for the battle she would probably have to fight to get a cab. In a mood verging on despair she wondered why she hadn't just ordered up a limo. Those guys wouldn't mind a dog, long as they got their fifty bucks. She searched the street for a gypsy cab, some line-jumper who'd just dropped somebody off and was willing to risk a quick passenger grab to avoid waiting. Then she saw a limo driver in his black suit holding up a card with her name on it: L. Ripken. He stood in front of a black Cadillac stretch limo. She went over. "I'm Lucy Ripken. Are you here for me?" Could it be possible? Her heart lifted. Her spirit soared.

"And a dog named Claud," the driver said. At that moment, the passenger door swung open, and from the depths of the car came a mock Eastern European voice.

"Velcome to my automobile, Ms. Ripken. And Monsieur Claud."

"Harry!" she cried, dropping her bags. "Harry, you made it!"

He leaped out of the back of the limo, and swept her into his arms. Claud instinctively rose up onto his hind legs, and they pulled him into the hug, two people and a dog embracing, while the driver carried Lucy's bags to the rear and loaded them into the trunk.

Shortly thereafter they were en route down the BQE, Lower–Manhattan-bound, Lucy drinking vodka, Harry drinking seltzer—he'd been on the wagon for a week now—and Claud on the carpeted floor, eating gourmet dog biscuits from a silver bowl. The stereo played late Talking Heads, music from Lucy's first years in New York, which she loved to hear every time she headed into town from the airport. They had finished with catch-up talk, and kissed enough times to know Harry would help her carry the bags up and stay the night unless he said something extremely stupid between now and then. He fished out the prints developed from the memory chip Lucy had sent him. She turned on a light and had a look at one—a transaction shot through the window of a Mexican house—then handed it to him. "So what else should I know about these dudes, Harry?" she asked.

He peered at the print. "Yep. Mon and Partridge. Doing a deal, eh? Nice surreptitious shooting, Luce, but you realize you are risking your butt here. These guys are major Texas bad boys. Dope, extortion, gun-running, maybe a little CIA back door contra work mixed in with the dope and guns, you know how the eighties went down there. These are the kind of people that leave bodies behind."

"Yeah, so I found out, Harry. A pair of serious sharks."

"Right. So you think they did in those art guys in Santa Fe, too? Jesus, I can't believe you tangled with these twisted fucks, Lucy!"

"I didn't plan on it, Harry. Swam right into it, know what I mean?"

"Happens, doesn't it?" He kissed her again, and her mouth opened against his. He tasted good, she wanted him, and he could smell her desire. "Meanwhile, I've been pining away, woman. My place or yours?"

She leaned back. "Hey, I've got a dog, Ipswich. And he's got to get used to his new pad. So, I guess Claud will permit your presence in his home. Although you might want to ask."

Harry looked at Claud, who lay on the car floor gnawing on a biscuit clutched between two paws. "Jesus, he looks like he could use a knife and fork. Hey, dog, can I come home with you?"

"Offer him a glass of champagne to wash his biscuit down, and perhaps he will allow it. He is a rather sophisticated beast," Lucy said, nose in the air as she scratched Claud's head. "Hey, what about Starfish? Isabel Chapin. You find anything on her?"

"Nothing other than that she and your friend Nathaniel Clements have been seen, sometimes together, sometimes apart, in most of the major drug towns in the Western hemisphere, usually during periods of high-intensity action. But she's never been popped. I think Nate's a little golden, thanks to Daddy, and some of it's rubbed off on her."

"You mean to say he's—what, protected?"

"Something like that. Just that he has generally been forewarned—when things were about to happen. As a matter of fact, some of my contacts with sources in the trade down there are convinced he's somebody's rat."

"Nate? Really?" Lucy asked, incredulous for about two seconds. "Actually, it makes perfect sense. He's definitely possessed of some rodent-like characteristics." She slipped her hand casually down into the neighborhood of Harry's crotch. "Hell of a horn player though," she added.

"So Nate Clements and that meta-bimbo Starfish have gotten themselves into the art trade, have they?" said Harry, gently placing a hand on her breast as they talked. He rubbed her softly. Harry did have wonderful hands, she remembered. She felt.

"Beats smuggling heroin, doesn't it?" Lucy said, somewhat breathless. Her nipples tingled under his fingertips. God, it had been a while.

"Yeah, I guess. But those two dead guys in Santa Fe might argue otherwise."

"Time to change the subject, Harry," she murmured, and licked gently at his earlobe.

Had the ride been from JFK they would have done it in the limo, but LaGuardia was too close to town. Before they could undress they were across the Williamsburg Bridge, zipping back up as they zipped down Delancey and Kenmare, around the corner onto Broome, and then home. They unloaded, Harry paid the man, Lucy drag-walked the bewildered dog around the block, and then she carried her purse and coaxed, pushed, and wheedled the poodle, who had never seen stairs before, while Harry hoisted all else up the endless, dusty, fluorescent-lit ninety-seven stairs that led to her home sweet home.

They ignored the blinking message light on the answering machine. They ignored the pile of mail on the floor, thrown there by her neighbor. They ignored the sound of a rat running from the room as they came in. They fell into a mad embrace on Lucy's bed, stripped each other quickly and deliberately, and soon commenced with an intense and satisfying fuck.

Afterward, they lay there completely exhausted and relaxed. Lucy now remembered why she kept Harry around.

Then and only then did she meander over to listen to her messages while sorting through the mail. Not bad: two checks in the mail adding up to thirteen hundred dollars. And a message from Rosa saying she was sorry they missed each other, and that she loved her, and that she would call again soon. Lucy, with a man she loved in her bed and Claud close by on the floor, went back to bed content, and stayed up late.

Saturday night in Manhattan, a week later. She and Harry had eaten at Spring Natural, sitting outside in the cool air so that Claud could hang out under the table. They contemplated going to a club, but instead bought the Sunday paper and walked back to the loft.

Harry, lounging on the bed at her side, scanned the Week in Review section. That was the male thing, right? She read the Arts and Leisure section and the back of the magazine, for food and fashion, while he read the front page. Now he turned to sports and she turned to the section requiring her most devoted concentration: the wedding announcements.

It had been a good week with Harry. Excellent, in truth. The sporadic nature of their affair, so dependent on his unannounced comings and goings, was becoming dependable in its own unpredictable fashion. Sure, he cut out of town without telling her on occasion, and she never knew how long he'd be gone. So what? He always came back, he usually brought her a present, and he'd been sober for two weeks now. Sober long enough to stop talking about being sober, which was a major step.

Time indeed to check the wedding announcements, which usually produced a sense of gnawing anxiety. At thirty-three, Lucy was far past the age of innocent dreams of wedded bliss, but that didn't mean she didn't have such dreams, or that she didn't need to read these announcements, simultaneously envious and superior as she checked the names and decoded the information.

She ran through them quickly, checking the photos, then the parentage, the wedding locations, her eye wandering back to the photos as she wondered about ages. Some of these girls and boys were way past debutante, that was certain. Don't give up, Luce, you might just make it. This is to announce the engagement of Lucy Delaney Ripken, daughter of Mr. and Mrs. Cyrus Ripken of Portland, Oregon, to Harold James Ipswich, son of Mr. and Mrs. Arthur Ipswich of Providence, Rhode Island. Ms. Ripken is a writer and photographer in New York City. Mr. Ipswich is a writer and an undercover narcotics agent, also based in New York City. The bride's parents will be unable to attend the wedding due to the fact that Mr. Ripken is an alcoholic and has no money and a bad attitude, and—What was this? Lucy's inevitably bitter little fantasy disappeared in a snap as her eyes were snagged by the four-part name under a photo of a sweet little blonde with a somehow familiar set of perfect white fangs. Ms. Camille Ariel Chapin Rooney, daughter of Mr. Arthur Rooney and Madeleine Chapin Rooney of Manhattan and Greenwich, Connecticut, whose wedding was scheduled for a day in June at a church in Greenwich, etc., etc.

Madeleine Chapin Rooney. Isabel Chapin? That's where she'd seen the name! On that bloody check that she'd cashed the day she'd gotten it, knowing full well the inevitability of her clash with Rooney. God, how could she have forgotten! Here was the missing link!

"Harry, look at this!" she said. "Madeleine Rooney's related to Starfish—Isabel Chapin, that is. I bet she's her damned aunt! These people are in it. This whole damn thing's a conspiracy."

Lucy tried calling Quentin and Beth Washington the next morning, and got a machine. She left an intentionally cryptic message, then called Beth's mother to see if they were visiting her. Beth's mom hemmed and hawed when

Lucy asked if she'd seen them; then, when Lucy identified herself, she was given a message: They'd gone to Martha's Vineyard, to a family cottage for a week or two. She got the number, called the Vineyard, and gave Quentin the latest. He said he planned to lie low until it all blew over, and also came up with his own contribution to the strategy, which they agreed to implement if and when necessary.

Lucy called Margaret. "Hey, Maggie, how's it going?"

"Lucy, that you? Not great. Weird phone calls coming in. In fact I almost didn't answer this one. Silent messages, heavy breathing and such. I've got Jedediah and his two sons doing guard duty up here. I think it's that Starfish gal again, but—"

"Where's Nathaniel?"

"Texas, with her, I guess. Told me he was coming up here soon as they got their deal done. Things are getting strange with him, Luce. He sounded really frightened last time we talked. I don't think he could really say anything, like somebody was listening or something."

"Probably our friends Jack and Lewis. Have you seen Rosa or Darren?"

"No. I think Rosa saw enough of me on that reef to last a lifetime, Lucy. Or at least a couple of months."

"Listen, I wanted to let you know—this thing is more complicated than I thought." Lucy filled her in.

Margaret decided to fly up to New York in a couple of days. "Why not?" she said. "Haven't been there in years, and the Waldorf's nice. Sounds like you could use the company. I could use the company, to tell the truth."

"You can stay here with me," Lucy said.

"Nah, I like New York hotels," Maggie said. "But I definitely want to spend some time. Be great to do the Apple with you, Luce. I haven't had a real friend living there in years. Have you ever been to The Four Seasons?"

"No way, honey. Out of my price range. And my neighborhood."

"Book a reservation for Thursday. You and me and Claud, is it?"

"No, Claud's the dog, Maggie. Harold's the man."

"Anyways, whichever one you want to bring, dinner's on me. See you Thursday, I'll call you when I get checked in."

"Sounds good." Lucy put the phone down and picked it up again to call Rosa.

Darren answered: "Hello?"

Lucy hung up without saying a word. Suddenly—or had this feeling been there all along?—she couldn't quite bring herself to trust him. If he had known Madeleine Chapin Rooney all those years, wouldn't he have known Isabel Chapin, or at least known of her?

Monday morning Lucy called her friend Nina Randolph, the editor of *Spaces* magazine. "Hey, Nina, it's Lucy. Lucy Ripken."

"Lucy. Hallo. How are you? Well, I trust." She was a formal sort, English transplant with that Brit reserve, but warm-hearted under the chill.

"Fine. Listen, I wanted to ask you a small favor. I just happened to have recently seen a really good-looking gallery renovation over on Madison I thought you might want to publish. I'm gonna shoot it on spec, just for you, because I am absolutely sure you are going to want it."

"So what's the catch?"

"No catch, really. I'll even eat the expenses. Just if a woman named Madeleine Rooney calls to verify that I'm shooting it for you, tell her it's true."

"That sounds manageable. I'll be happy to view the pictures once you've shot them, Lucy."

"I'll send you a set of transparencies next week."

Next came the trickier call—to Madeleine Rooney. She wouldn't be there on a Monday, but Lucy could leave a message and hope she'd call back. The machine answered. "Hello, Madeleine, this is Lucy Ripken. I'm back from New Mexico—and from Mexico—and I have some interesting things to talk about. Please call me ASAP when you get this message."

She and Claud ran down the stairs. The sun was out and spring was everywhere blooming in the busy streets of SoHo. She leashed him and walked to the park at Spring and Mulberry. The alcoholics who usually occupied most of the benches were still sleeping it off somewhere, so she sat with coffee and a paper while Claud chased pigeons on a peaceful Monday morning in New York City, bright flowers in window boxes and on fire escapes, no truck engines idling at a roar for the moment, and no lunatics, village idiots, or piles of garbage in her range of vision. Harry had left early for the airport with some business to take care of down in Florida, but he'd promised to be back by the end of the week. He'd even told her where he was going. Now that was a sign.

Back at the loft there was one message, from Madeleine Rooney, with a phone number. Lucy called. "Hello, Madeleine, it's Lucy Ripken." She kept her voice carefully neutral.

"Lucy. Yes. You called?"

"I wanted to congratulate you on your daughter's wedding. I saw the announcement."

"Thank you. So, what have you got to say for yourself now that you've done your little thing down in Santa Fe, Ms. Ripken?"

"By the way, is your niece Isabel going to be attending the wedding?"

She didn't miss a beat. "Isabel? What are you talking about? Who's Isabel?"

"Well, she goes by the name of Starfish these days."

"My daughter's wedding guest list is certainly no concern of yours, Ms. Ripken. Now, did you have something to discuss regarding my artifacts?"

"Actually, I wanted to make amends, in a manner of speaking. I'm right in the middle of my article, and I'm not sure where it's going, to tell the truth, but I will let you know if you're going to be in the story, Mrs. Rooney. I will do that much." Lucy waited for a reaction. Rooney said nothing. Lucy went on. "Anyways, I am a freelancer. I write and photograph stories for design magazines on a regular basis, and I was wondering if you would be interested in having the gallery photographed for *Spaces* magazine? I think I told you before how much I admired the interior. Great finishes—I love the notion of old west style gone uptown and laid on top of a classical space plan, with great art lighting. It would look marvelous in a design book."

"Thanks. *Spaces*? I've seen that magazine. My designer showed me some copies when we were planning the remodel here."

"Good. Then perhaps you'd be interested in a feature on the gallery?"

"What will it cost me?"

"Nothing but some time, since I assume you'll want to be there when I shoot. By the way, who was the designer of the space?"

"Enrico Lobos. He's a marvelous young man from Miami. His parents are Nicaraguans who left after the Sandinistas took over. He was recommended to me by a friend. I'm sure he would be thrilled to be in *Spaces*. But I want it in writing that I will have no expenses incurred. When did you want to do the photography?"

"When's the next day you're closed? Sunday?"

"Yes."

"Sunday then, if that's okay. I'll be there, with my equipment and an assistant, around eight in the morning. Is that all right?"

"I'll be here."

"We can discuss the situation with the artifacts at greater length at that time, Mrs. Rooney. Please try to have the gallery as clean and neat as possible, okay?"

"Is that nice young man Simon going to be assisting you?"

"If he's available, I'll book him."

Madame Rooney hung up. Lucy put the phone down, wondering why that call had been so painless. The lady seemed so unconcerned. A week ago she's threatening my ass, and now she's, like, strictly business, sort of bored about it all. Weird.

Thursday afternoon the phone rang with that special ring that signaled an important call. Sure it was Maggie calling from the airport, Lucy leapt for the phone and had it to her ear before the first ring finished. "Maggie, is that you? Are you here?"

"Lucy? It's Rosa. My God, Lucy."

"Rosa? Hey, honey, I'm sorry, it's just that Maggie's due in town today and—"

"I don't think so. Lucy, Nathaniel's dead, and Maggie—Margaret's—"

"What?" she shrieked.

"I've been calling up there to her house, I wanted to see her, and no one answered the phone for, like, three days, so we went up there this morning, me and Darren. The front door was open, all the animals were running loose, Maggie was gone, and we found Nathaniel in the house. He'd been shot in the back."

"Shot in the back? By whom? Who would—"

"You know who would do it, Luce. It had to be—It has to be those guys. They're here in Santa Fe, Lucy."

"Where's Maggie?"

"Darren found her Rolodex open to her travel agent, so we called him. She had a ticket to New York but she traded it in for a ticket to London and from there to Nairobi. She's gone to Africa, Lucy. I think she's just hiding. On the run."

"Africa! Jesus. That's a long way to run. Have you seen the bitch?"

"Starfish? No. If she's around she's laying low. She and her crazy killer friends. We should have nailed her when we had a chance, Lucy. They might be after me next, for God's sake!"

"What are you going to do?"

"We're going to San Francisco tonight, to stay with Darren's parents, if I can talk that cop Rodriguez into letting us leave. He's a little leery since this is the second time we've called him to report we walked in on dead people in the last two weeks."

"Just go. If you're not suspects he can't make you stay, Rosa. Just get the fuck out of there. Christ, that poor fool Nathaniel."

"I feel badly for him, but frankly, Lucy, I'm more concerned with myself at the moment. He's already dead, know what I mean?"

"Do I ever. Be careful. Darren okay?"

"Sure, he's fine. I mean, he's not too happy about having to sneak out of town like this, but he understands."

"Call me from S.F."

"I will. Take care."

7

Broken Dreams and Broken Statues

In a Checker Cab, cruising up Park Avenue through sparse Sunday morning traffic, Lucy headed back to the Desert Gallery. Much had changed. For this shoot, along with Simon Stevens she'd hired a second assistant, one Harold Ipswich, forty-four-year-old loverboy, undercover DEA man, and travel writer. After she'd taken Claud for an early stroll on Crosby Street, Harold and Simon had hauled the equipment downstairs and two blocks over to Lafayette Street, where they'd grabbed a northbound cab. There was less gear this time around as well, since she planned to shoot $2^1/4$ transparencies and had left home the 4 x 5 camera. Familiar now with the space, she knew she wouldn't need supplementary lighting. The banks of bright white MR-16s would do the job.

They stopped in front of the gallery, and the men unloaded while she went to the glass doors and peered in. The buzzer sounded and she pushed the door open. Madeleine Rooney, in a bright red jumpsuit, gold-bejeweled, with a cigarette in hand, floated toward her. "Good morning, Lucy. You're ten minutes late." The tone was strictly business. She blew smoke at Lucy.

"Sorry about that."

"I can only stay till noon. Can you get it done?"

"You said two p.m. on the phone."

"My plans have changed. Surely four hours is enough time. In any case, it will have to do."

"Fine. We'll work fast." Lucy held the door as Simon, followed by Harold, lugged gear from the cab. Simon grinned at Mrs. Rooney.

"Hiya, Madeleine," he said.

"Good morning, Simon." She smiled. Her smile went away when she saw Harold. Harold had a troubled aura, as they might say in Santa Fe. "Who's this?"

"Harold Ipswich," Lucy said. "I brought a second assistant so we could work faster. Seemed like a good idea, and so it is, since we're in a rush, eh? Harold, meet Madeleine Rooney. Madeleine, Harold Ipswich."

"Hello," said Harold. Lucy hoped he would contain his inherent hostility toward the Rooney type. "Nice place you got here," he added, looking past her.

"Hello." Rooney ignored his outstretched hand. "Lucy, could you step into the office a minute? I need a word."

"You guys want to get out the camera and tripod and set up?" Lucy said. She looked around. "Si, see if you can figure out the best angle for this room. Looks like thataway." She pointed. "From over here. I'll be back in a minute." She followed Rooney into the office.

"Sit down," said Madeleine, waving at the chair facing her glass-topped desk. Lucy sat. Madeleine threw a brochure on the desk and sat down behind it, put out her smoke, and lit another. "Here's the catalogue. I thought you might want to see the results of your work."

Lucy picked it up. Sleek, expensive stock, four-color printing, an auction date a few days away. She riffled through. Along with some items she didn't recognize, the six pieces she'd photographed were there, in living lovely color, with brief italic descriptions beneath. Full provenance and certification available. She'd done a good job; the pictures looked great. The pieces looked great. The whole nine yards. Sleek and professional and full of lies. "So, you're going to go ahead and have your sale, in spite of the authenticity question."

"That's what I wanted to talk to you about," Madeleine said. "The sale's been cancelled. The pieces were stolen the night before last."

"Stolen? From here?" Lucy stared at the woman, who looked back steadily. "Are you serious? Someone broke in here and took them?" Lucy couldn't keep a smirk off her face. This was too much.

"They jimmied the back door and de-activated the alarm system. First time I've been robbed in the eight years I've been in business. The police were here yesterday. They dusted for fingerprints but it looks like it was a professional job. That's why I needed to talk to you. You'll be hearing from my insurance company, because you were one of the few people who actually saw the pieces on the premises. Believe me when I tell you I had no interest in your getting involved in this, but when the adjuster saw the photographs yesterday—I had to show them to him so he could verify the pieces—he insisted that he wanted to talk to you. His name is Wyatt. Kelly Wyatt. He works for Brueton Insurance International. He'll be getting in touch."

"But you realize I have to tell him what I know, Mrs. Rooney. I have to tell him the truth. The pieces are forgeries."

"That may be your opinion, but it's not what Herman Forte and the letters of authentication and the appraisal say, Lucy," she said. "Would you like to see the letters?"

"Those letters are bogus, Madeleine, you know that. Don't tell me you're not aware of what happened to the men who wrote them."

"I'm not interested in what happened to them. I have legal documentation on the pieces, and now they've been stolen."

"What about Quentin and Beth? They're not going to sit back and let this bullshit fly."

"I don't think Quentin's really interested in sticking his nose into this affair at this point, Lucy," Rooney said, and gave her a look. "He has enough to worry about with his family, and that new job he's hoping to land."

"I wouldn't be so sure about that," said Lucy, but she knew the woman had a point. Quentin had a lot to lose, as he'd been reminded. "Even if you're right, Madeleine, I may not be an expert like Beth or Quentin, but I know more about this situation than anybody else."

Madeleine looked her in the eye. "Yes, well—Lucy, would you agree that the photography work you're doing for me today is worth, say, twenty-five thousand?"

"Twenty-five grand? Are you serious?" Lucy stopped herself. Jesus, she could get a lot done with that kind of cash. But it's blood money, for God's sake. "Madeleine, just how much insurance do you have on those pieces?"

She didn't hesitate. "A million dollars' worth, Lucy."

So that's why Rooney had chosen to let her shoot the space! Drag her into the scheme, buy her off, and shut her up. Lucy felt a momentary bewilderment—not over whether or not to accept, that was out of the question, but over how to proceed. How to nail the brazen bitch! And with her, her band of murderous cronies. They had to be in it together. "Let me think this over," she said, buying time. "I don't know."

"Tomorrow by noon I want an answer. You have my home phone number. Now, why don't you go ahead and take your pictures." Madeleine Rooney was a tiny dame, but she puffed herself up way large to make her next pronouncement: "And keep in mind, Lucy, that I have the testimony of Dr. Herman Forte; certified letters of authentication; a certified, legal appraisal; a flawless history with my insurance company since I've never made a claim; and ten years of hard-earned reputation behind me. What, pray tell, do you have, aside from your own little story and your friends Quentin and Beth Washington, who seem to have disappeared from the face of the earth? Perhaps Quentin's gone back to Texas to rejoin the drug trade. What do you think?"

By the time they finished shooting their transparencies three hours later, Lucy did have something to enhance her most potent weapon, the truth. Harold had planted a voice-activated bug on the underside of a display pedestal close to the door to the office in the back of the gallery. They packed up and left the gallery, found a cab and sent Simon home with the gear, then waited in the coffee shop up the block. As soon as Rooney left the gallery, they went back down the block and Harold flashed some twenties and quickly finagled a little room in the basement of the building next door, where he installed his surveillance gear. Every call Madeleine Rooney made or received would be recorded on a machine set up in that room. Harold even jury-rigged a telephone line and stuck in a phone. Lucy decided she liked having a lover in the DEA. He had all kinds of useful tricks up his sleeve.

She called the surveillance room at seven the next morning. No answer. Where the hell was Harold? She tried his home phone. Nothing. After taking Claud over to the park on the East River for a run, she hiked down Broadway to the pool and took a swim—her first since crossing the channel, and she wallowed with delight in the fluorescent-lit, heavily chlorinated pool water, so very, very safe and close to shore. Then she took the train up the east side. The gallery was closed, it being Monday. She used the key

Harold had given her to get into the basement next door. The room stunk of rats. It appeared that Harold had not been back.

A blinking red light on the machine told her the phone had been used. Lucy took out the tape and put a new one in its place. She left the building and went home.

At home she put the tape in her little recorder, then took a seat at her desk for a listen. The first call was Madeleine Rooney discussing wedding plans with her daughter, ingrown family arguments about a wedding dress and a caterer. The second call was someone calling about the auction. Madeleine explained that it had been cancelled. The third call went like this:

"Hi, Maddy, it's me." A familiar voice, but whose?

"Hello. Good you called back. Can we talk?"

"Yes, she's playing tennis with Mother."

"I don't think LR's going to go for it."

"Are you serious? She doesn't have any money. Offer more."

"It has to come from your share, then."

Hesitation. "Fine. Okay. Another ten enough?"

"We'll see. She's supposed to call me at home at noon tomorrow."

"What about our friends? You know they followed us up here."

"Put them off a little longer."

"Put them off! Jesus, Maddy, they're scary. They want their money. Christ, you're the one that got us tangled up with them. That damned Starfish—"

"Her name is Isabel."

"Whatever. She's brought us nothing but trouble. She told me they were just trying to scare Rosa and them out there, but that's not what Rosa told me, Maddy."

"Look, I didn't want to get them involved, either. But we needed them to do what had to be done, and they did it, right? Now we have to deal with it. Once they get their money they'll leave us alone. But we've got to tough it out till then. We have no choice."

"I know, Maddy, but—"

"Why don't you sic them on LR? She's really our only problem at this point."

"Because she's one of Rosa's best friends, and I don't want her hurt unless we have no choice."

"Well, I don't know what she's going to say to the man at the insurance company, but she's certainly a nosy bitch. I hope there aren't any real surprises. If there are, well—I may have to send for those guys to come up here. You are aware of that, I trust?"

"We've said too much already, Maddy. I think I'd better go."

"If she calls Rosa, try to find out what she's planning to do. We need to know."

"Jesus, Maddy, aren't we in deep enough already?" he whined.

She hung up on him. Lucy turned the machine off, moved to the couch, lay down, and closed her eyes. She tried to relax but she was too jumpy. What a mess! Darren in it up to his eyeballs.

Just shy of eleven a.m. She had an hour. She called Harold. "Hello?" he slurred into the phone after a single ring. Damn, she thought. She knew that tone. But she couldn't stop herself from needing him, believing in him.

"Hi, it's me."

"Lucy, how ya doin'? What'sappening?" Yep, no doubt about it, he was drunk. Fuck!

"Harold, what are you doing drunk on Monday morning?" she said, beginning calmly. "I need your help with something, and you're all fucked up!"

He was silent for a moment. "Damn," he said. "Hey, sorry, Luce. Iss just that I fergodda tell you. Today's the anniversary of the day my brother died. Remember I tol' you how me and my brother were so close, we were—"

"Junkies together, and then he OD'ed and you left him there. Yeah, Harold, I remember the whole sad story. And do you remember, you selfish prick, that I needed your help today with something really important, and you are all messed up and can't help me. So piss off," she shouted, and slammed the phone down, bursting into tears. "Asshole," she said, then saw Claud cowering. "Hey, I'm sorry, baby," she said to the dog. "If there's anything in the world I have no patience with, it's a drunken man," she said. "I don't care what the excuse is, but—oh, never mind," she sighed. "Come here, baby. I'm sorry I yelled." Claud came over and lay down on the couch next to her, and she hugged him, and for a moment let herself go and cried.

The phone rang. After eight rings, she lifted and dropped the receiver. Her estimate was that he would try once more, and then give up and not call back until he got sober.

She called Brueton Insurance and asked for Kelly Wyatt. She got him on the phone and set up an appointment to discuss the Desert Gallery situation at one that day.

At noon she called Madeleine Rooney at home. "Hello, Madeleine, it's Lucy."

"Yes."

"I have film for you to look at."

"Fine. What about the payment we discussed for the work?"

"I wanted to talk to you about that. Can we meet at the gallery later today? Say, three o'clock?"

"Why not sooner?"

"Because I'm seeing Mr. Kelly Wyatt at one, and I don't know how long that conversation is going to last."

Rooney took that in. "Three, then."

Lucy packed up her assorted photographs, pocketed the re-wound tape, and left, stopping by the lab to pick up the three sets of transparencies she'd ordered from the shoot yesterday. She arranged to have a messenger deliver one to Nina Randolph at *Spaces*. Got to keep working, whatever else happens. Then she got on the uptown train in time to make her one o'clock with Kelly Wyatt at Brueton Insurance International. En route she had a look at the transparencies. The gallery gleamed with funky elegance. It looked better than in real life. She'd done a good job. She would see this story in *Spaces*, and make some money off the shoot. Maybe eight hundred instead of twenty-five thousand, but at least they'd be honest bucks.

The Brueton offices were located in an anonymous midtown east building, and Wyatt's cubicle was as anonymous as the block and the building. Wyatt himself was thirtyish and hip in appearance, with his little black ponytail and his black leather jacket, black T-shirt, and black cowboy boots with silver toetips. But then again, he specialized in the art market, and trendiness was a requisite. Even at the insurance end of it.

After they'd gone through the preliminaries and made some simpatico small talk about the downtown scene, which he obviously prided himself on being a part of even if he did work at a midtown insurance company, Lucy laid her images out on his desk. She told her convoluted tale, utilizing pictures to illustrate each narrative point, beginning with the photos of the works in the gallery and ending with the tape she'd just listened to. As she ran it by him, she watched Wyatt's face. He didn't look convinced.

When she finished, he sat for a minute, drumming his fingers on the desk. Without speaking he looked over the pictures again. Dead bodies floating in a pool. A woman prancing nude on a terrace wall. Little statues here, and there, and everywhere. He looked at her, and at last he spoke: "You know, Lucy, this claim is going to cost Brueton a million bucks, so believe me, I would like to find this story plausible. I would love to find grounds to reject Madeleine Rooney's claim. But let's try to be objective. First of all, let me say that it is an interesting tale, one way or the other. I'll grant you that. But, to cut to the chase, I have to assume that you made that tape surreptitiously. I don't know how and I don't want to, but—it is an illegal and therefore useless piece of evidence, any way you look at it. Plus, without your story to back it up, it doesn't really say much. A couple of people talking about some stuff—I don't know, strange but—not exactly prosecutable, know what I mean? Not to me anyway, and in saying that I'm speaking for the company. In fact, none of these photographs say much. I mean, there are some eye-catching images here, and you put them all together, and you weave your tangled tale, and it sounds sort of convincing, but—I'll be honest with you—I'm simply not convinced. Madeleine Rooney is just too Madison Avenue to be involved in this kind of stuff, Lucy. I mean, her husband is on the board at the Whitney, for God's sake! Plus, and I'll be frank with you—I know you're a journalist working on a story about this, so you are not entirely objective. And I know you have some marginally flaky friends you want to offer up as expert witnesses. And I also happen to know that you are involved with a guy who is an undercover narcotics agent—and Madeleine Rooney knows all about him. I would guess that he's the party responsible for that tape you played for me, and frankly, she's ready to blow his cover if she must. Don't ask me how she found out, I don't know anything about it, but she comes from a world of connections, Lucy, connections that go so high you can't imagine. And she's been paying her premiums faithfully for, like, ten years, and has never once made a claim. So, what am I to do with this?" He waved at the piles of prints and transparencies. "What do you want from me?"

"What do I want from you?" Lucy said, and leveled a look at him. "I'm talking about murder, Wyatt, and you're talking about connections! I want you to help me prove the truth."

"Two HIV-positive gay men, and an alcoholic musician known to be a small-time drug dealer and a chronic gambler. Call it two sad but understandable suicides and a case of bad karma catching up to a born loser."

"I can't believe you," Lucy said, standing up and shoving her evidence back into the envelope. "What, are you on the Rooney payroll, too? Is that it? I'm trying to get a little justice, stop some bad people, and save your company a million bucks, and you aren't even interested. You stupid fool." Lucy whirled and walked toward the door, fighting back tears.

"Tell you what, Lucy." She stopped in the doorway and turned around. "I'll do this much for you: I'll get a one-week hold on the claim payment. But that's all I can manage. This company has made its reputation in part by fast payment on claims. See what else you can come up with. If what you've got is all there is, next Monday the money's hers. I'll probably be hung by my toes for doing this much. And Lucy, a question: If you don't think the pieces got stolen, what do you suppose she did with them?"

"Good question," she said. "Thanks." She dashed out. Well, thank God for small favors. Christ, it had all seemed so clear to her. Murder to cover up a forgery hustle, more murder to cover up an insurance hustle, murders and hustles all bound together in the neat little package represented by her photographs and her narrative. She had the written version at home on the computer, backed up on a disk hidden in her underwear drawer. She'd just tried the oral version out on a captive audience, and he hadn't been an easy sell.

After downing some noodles in a Japanese fast food joint she tried Quentin on the Vineyard from a phone booth. No answer. Where were the missing pieces? Probably in smithereens in the Dumpster in back of the Desert Gallery. No, Rooney probably saved them to give for Christmas presents. After all, they were pretty, and worth a couple hundred bucks each.

She had talked herself back into a relatively confident mode by the time she reached the gallery, where La Rooney lay waiting, eager to snare Lucy in her web. Lucy contemplated sneaking around back to inspect the trash before approaching the front door, but decided that Rooney might be ruthless but she wasn't stupid.

Rooney buzzed her in, remaining in her little power spot, enveloped in a protective cloud of toxic smoke behind the counter in back. Lucy approached, envelope in hand. "Hello, Madeleine, here's your set of transparencies." Lucy tossed them on the counter.

Rooney pulled them out and had a look. "Oh, they're lovely, just lovely. I can't wait to show them to Enrico, he's going to be so thrilled. Do you want to talk with him? I mean, about the design?" She coughed without bothering to cover her mouth.

"Yes, of course," Lucy said. "When the article is scheduled I'll need to interview him."

"And here's your payment," Rooney said, pushing a check across the counter as if they had planned it this way all along. Lucy picked it up. Twenty-five thousand dollars, made out to her. "Photography expenses" on the memo line.

Lucy had a good long look, for drama's sake, then tore the check neatly in half and dropped it on the counter. "I want more," she said.

"What do you mean?"

"Like you and Darren discussed. Another ten would be nice."

"What are you talking about?" Rooney went momentarily white under her Palm Beach winter tan and her makeup. She put out her cigarette, fished another from a gold case, and lit the wrong end. Then put it out and got it right the second time.

"Just this." Lucy pulled out her mini-tape recorder and turned it on. This was her third listen. She practically had it memorized. At the end of the conversation, she turned it off. "So how about another ten grand?"

Madeleine looked at her carefully. "I think that can be arranged. Assuming you let me have that tape. Not that there's anything on there that particularly concerns me," she quickly added. "Besides, you and I both know it was illegally recorded."

"Now what would make you think such a thing?"

"You have to get a warrant to tap phones, Lucy. There's no way on earth you could have one. Of course you will have to call Mr. Wyatt back and tell him to forget that week's delay on my payment you convinced him to give you for your idiotic little investigation. But, just to save time, I'm willing to up your photographic charges another ten thousand dollars."

"Right now?"

"In exchange for that tape."

"What if there are copies? What about my photographs? What about my article?"

"I don't think you made copies." She was right. "And none of that other business matters to me now, Lucy. I just want my insurance payment, understand?" She pulled out her check book. Lucy pocketed the tape recorder, tape still inside, and headed toward the door.

"Your pictures are on the counter there. I'll let you know when I need to reach Mr. Lobos." She stopped at the door and pushed it open. "Just one other thing I was curious about: Where did you stash the 'stolen' pieces? At your house, or at your husband's office, or where?" She didn't allow Rooney time to answer. She went out, quickly found a taxi, then blasted home.

She made a few fast calls and on the third one scored, talking her downstairs neighbor Jane into feeding and walking Claud for a couple of days. Then she packed an overnight bag and took off for the airport, San Francisco–bound. From the airport she called home just before boarding, and changed her message to say that she was headed down to the Yucatán on assignment.

She'd have liked Harry to be there, watching out for Claud and the rest of her life while she traveled, but he was a drunk and unreliable. That was a true fact and though she loved him, she'd have to get used to it, or give him up.

The way she'd figured it, she could hunt the goods, but that would be tough. The "stolen" pieces could be anywhere in the greater Manhattan area, stashed in a country house in Connecticut, or wasted in the Fresh Kills Landfill, transformed, dust to dust. Or she could go after the bad guys, but this meant waiting for Harry to sober up, for she would need some quasi-legal, or at least quasi-professional, help from him and his resources. She did not want to try to bag Partridge and Mon, or even the fish woman, on her own. They were true believers in the right to keep and bear arms, and to use them. And Harry was drunk.

Instead she had made this choice: to attempt rescue of her friend from a disastrous relationship, and in doing so, possibly bring down one of the people responsible for the deaths of three men. One of the bad guys. But Darren did not qualify, somehow, as a bona fide bad guy. He was just enough of a sap to have let himself stumble into circumstances beyond his control. Lucy sighed. She would have to break Rosa's heart this very day.

She landed at the San Francisco airport late in the afternoon, and called the parents' house. A man answered the phone. Lucy asked for Rosa, and she came on a minute later. "Hi, Rose, it's me. Who was that, the butler?"

"Lucy, how are you? What great timing! I have some wonderful news!"

"What's that?"

"We're getting married. I mean, right away. We decided why wait? Can you get out here in a couple of weeks? It's gonna be June eleventh, here at Darren's parents' place."

"I'm here now, Rosa."

"What do you mean? You're in San Francisco? What's going on?" The anxiety surfaced in her voice. "Lucy, does this have something to do with—you know, Mexico, and the art?"

"Yeah, it does, honey. It definitely does. And to do with you, too. Listen, I don't want to beat around the bush, Rosa. It's too serious. Can we meet for dinner in town?"

Rosa hesitated. "Darren too?"

"No. And if you don't mind, I wish you wouldn't tell him I'm here. I have my reasons. I've got to talk to you alone, Rosa."

"Lucy, what are you up to now? I'll have to make excuses. Dinner's a pretty formal event around here."

"Do what you have to. Please, Rosa, I wouldn't be here if it wasn't—look, you know that new restaurant with the voluptuous purple velvet and gilt interiors, supposed to be the hottest spot in town?"

"Mohair Mohawk? Yeah, in fact Darren's father is a partner. We go there all the time."

"Forget it, then. I don't want to see anyone you know."

"You familiar with the Tadich Grill?"

"Yeah."

"Let's meet there and have dinner. I'll figure out an excuse to get out of here. Seven o'clock. And Lucy, whatever you have to tell me, don't mess with my marriage plans, because they are not going to change, I don't care what the hell you tell me," she said defiantly.

"See you at seven." Lucy put down the phone, hailed a cab, and headed into town, depressed. Lucy the homewrecker was thirty-three years old. Rosa was several years younger but she had practically given up on getting married until she met Darren.

Lucy checked into a budget hotel off Market Street, freshened up, and walked to the Tadich, a bit of a hike but she had half an hour and an unhappy task ahead. She strode quickly through the cool evening air, and felt quite warm by the time she reached the restaurant. She hadn't been in San Francisco in years, but she had hardly noticed the city around her.

Rosa was sitting at the bar nursing what looked like a straight vodka. Lucy approached her. "Hi, Rosita," she said, and gave her a kiss on the cheek. "How're you doing?"

Rosa's response was half-hearted. "I'm okay, Luce. Or should I say, I was great until you called, and now I don't know. So let's cut the bullshit. What's the story?"

"Nobody knows you're here?"

"I told them I was going to a movie. Darren was playing basketball with some college buds. Kind of nice staying with the family, getting dinners cooked and all. His mom's actually really sweet."

"Let's get a booth. Are you hungry? A glass of pinot noir, please," she said to the bartender.

"Not really."

"Well, we need privacy." The bartender poured her wine, and they moved to a booth. As soon as they were seated Lucy got out her tape player and set it on the table.

"What's this?" Rosa asked.

"A tape I want you to hear. I'm going to say this now, because I know you're going to be upset. Just listen, Rosa, and remember this isn't my fault. I'm sorry."

"Just play the bloody thing, Lucy, for God's sake!" Rosa said. Lucy turned it on. She'd erased the first two conversations, so the Darren/Rooney conversation began immediately. They listened in silence all the way through, Lucy watching Rosa, who stared at the tape recorder.

When it was over, Lucy turned it off, and looked at her friend's face. Rosa stared back at her, in a kind of shock. Their eyes locked. Behind Rosa's eyes, a world was crumbling.

"What—who was—" She stopped, and looked at Lucy imploringly. "Tell me that wasn't Darren, Lucy. Please. Tell me."

"I'm sorry, honey." Tears were flowing down her cheeks. "I didn't want to do this, but—"

"Where did you get that—why did—who made that tape? Jesus, Lucy, do you know what you've done?"

"I didn't plan it this way, Rosey. I was going after Madeleine Rooney. After Nathaniel died, and then the so-called robbery in New York, I didn't know what else to do."

"Robbery? What robbery?"

Why would he have told her? "The pieces that I photographed—the fakes—were stolen a couple of days ago. Madeleine Rooney had them insured for a million dollars. She's about to collect the money, and I had to—have to stop her."

"Why? What in the hell makes you—why is it your job to stick your neck right into the middle of this? Jesus, Lucy, Darren's—"

"He's involved, Rosa. He got involved with Madeleine Rooney, setting up the Precolombian deal. Then when they turned out to be fakes—that was Nathaniel's little scam, and I don't think anybody knew about it at that point except maybe Starfish. But they ended up using those Dallas thugs to do their dirty work. They found those guys through Starfish, I guess. And she's related to Madeleine Rooney, Rosa! But they . . . they hired those guys, so they're accessories to murder."

"Murder? You're telling me Darren is involved in murder?"

"You heard the tape, Rosa. He knows exactly who killed Hamilton Walking Wind, and Calvin Hobart, and Nathaniel Clements. My God, Rosa, he's still doing business with them after they tried to kill us. Rosa, I'm sorry, but for whatever reason, he got involved, and he's up to his neck in it. You've got to get out of here."

"But I'm getting married, Lucy."

"Rosa, I can't tell you how sorry I am about this, but you simply cannot marry this guy. I know it's your dream, but he's going to be taking a fall. He's probably going to be going to prison. Unless they kill me first, I have to nail Rooney, and I can't see any way that he isn't going to go down with her." Lucy took Rosa's hands. "Look, I've booked two seats on a red-eye out of here. Tonight. You can't stay here."

"I have to talk to him, Lucy. I'm sure there's a reason for—I know he didn't mean to—"

"All he meant to do was make some money. Nothing wrong with that. I don't even want to get into the ethics of the forgery scam, Rosa, because to tell the truth I don't really give a shit if the fucking hunks of clay are five days old or five hundred years old. But when they started knocking people off it turned into a different deal. One way or another Darren could have backed off at that point, and he chose not to."

"Stop it. Just stop it, Lucy. Please." Rosa went cold. "So, what do you propose? I fly back with you? And then what? What about my life in Santa Fe?"

"You're going to have to start over. You can stay with me in New York, or you can find a different place in Santa Fe, you just do what you have to do, but what you have to do now is get out of this mess before he drags you down with it."

Lucy carried in her purse a ten grain valium for occasions such as this. She split it with Rosa in the cab en route to the airport, and so they both zoned out intermittently across the midnight skies of America. Lucy heard Rosa's muffled crying in her waking moments, and it brought tears to her eyes as well. This was a sad thing she had done. Life was cruel at times, and this was one of them.

They arrived home a little before noon, having wasted a couple of groggy hours laying over in Detroit. They passed Rosa's old loft building a moment before reaching Lucy's corner. "Looks as grubby as ever around here," Rosa said as they got out of the cab.

"Nothing's really changed," Lucy said. "The restaurant across the street went out of business, the Cuban cafe got shut down for running a casino in the basement, and two people I know got mugged on Crosby last month."

"Jesus," said Rosa. "So nice to be back."

They went upstairs. The message light was blinking fast.

The first from Maggie. "Lucy, are you really in Mexico? Well, I'm back. Here in the Apple, I mean. I'm staying where I told you I would be. Call me when you get this."

The second from Kelly Wyatt. "Ms. Ripken, I have some interesting news for you. Please call me ASAP. Thanks."

The third and fourth were hang-ups. The fifth was Harold. He sounded worn, contrite as hell. "Lucy, it's me. I know, I fucked up, I'm sorry, you probably never want to speak to me again, but call me when you do."

The sixth was Madeleine Rooney. "Ms. Ripken, our deal is off! Off, you hear me? I don't know what the hell you told that insurance adjuster, but if things don't change fast you are going to be extremely sorry you ever—Do you hear me?—ever stuck your nose into my business. Is that perfectly clear? You'll be hearing from me." Slam.

The seventh was another hang-up. The eighth was from San Francisco. "Hello, Lucy, goddammit where are you? This is Darren and I know you—I just know you've—Rosa, are you there, Rosa did you go back to Mexico with her? Honey, don't believe that woman, she's got her own agenda, she wants to break us up, she's just jealous, you can't believe her. Please call me, honey, please." He sobbed for a moment. "Please call. It's midnight. I love you, Rosa. Please come home." He hung up.

"Lucy, I've got to call him," Rosa said. "I've got to." She picked up the phone.

"Don't do it, Rosa. Not now. It's too late." Rosa looked at her, and dropped the phone on the floor. She sat heavily on the sofa, put her head in her hands, and began crying softly.

"God, I am so sorry, Rosie," Lucy said, sitting by her and stroking her hair. "I am so sorry."

The next message was from Quentin. "Lucy, you can't be—what are you, crazy? If you're crazy you're in Mexico, and if you're not crazy, when you get this message call me at Martha's."

The last message was another one from Harold. "Listen, Lucy, I don't know if you're in Mexico or not, but I can tell you who are: your friends Louie and Jackie and Starbaby. My sources are impeccable, and your pals are Merida-bound from San Francisco. My guess is they heard your machine message and headed down thataways to try to run you down. So if you're down there, baby, watch your tail, and call me when you get back. I love you, like I said before, I'm sorry. Baby please, baby please, baby baby baby please."

"Bingo!" Lucy said, and called the Vineyard. Quentin answered on the second ring. "Lucy?"

"Yeah, it's me. Time for Plan B."

"You mean they're down there?"

"I'm here in New York, and they're all three en route to Merida from San Francisco, probably after me. That's why I put that message on my machine, Quentin. Run a little interference, buy some time, see if the bad boys would go for it. They did. So I guess it's time for you to do what you have to."

"You sure you want to do this?" As he'd explained before, through art world circles Quentin knew the curator who ran the private museum for the millionaire drug dealer in Merida. As Quentin pointed out, this nouveau riche dope dealer would be quite pleased to nail a trio of lowlife gringos who had ripped him off at least once already, and were intent on doing so again. Like most Mexican millionaires, even gringo ones, the guy was well connected with the Federales, and could easily arrange to have the three busted for smuggling contraband, Precolombian artifacts, whatever it took to earn them some down time in a Mexican prison.

"We haven't got any choice. If they come up here they're going to be on my case and yours until they take a fall or we do. And they are serious bad boys, Quentin. You know that."

"Yeah. Okay, I'll make the call."

"Let me know if there's a problem. Otherwise, I'd just as soon not hear another word, know what I mean?"

"Sure. So what's the latest with Madam Madeleine?"

"You heard about the so-called theft?"

"Yeah. What a transparent scam."

"Really. But apparently the insurance company bought it, last I heard. Although there's a message here from the guy there, who wants me to call. It sounds like maybe he's wised up, I don't know."

"Keep me posted."

"Likewise."

Lucy called Kelly Wyatt. "Hello, it's Lucy Ripken. You called me?"

"Yes I did. I have some rather momentous news. Can you make it in here today? Like ASAP?"

"What's the story?"

"I can't discuss it over the phone."

"I'll be there in—let's see, it's nearly one. Around three okay?"

"Copacetic." He hung up.

"Copacetic?" She looked at the phone. "God, I hate that word." She looked at Rosa, numb on the sofa. "Want to take a ride uptown, honey?" she said while calling information and getting the number for the Waldorf.

"Sure," Rosa said dully. "Why not?"

Lucy got Maggie on the phone. "Hey, was I glad to hear from you or what?" Lucy said.

"You're in New Yawk? You're back from Mexico?"

"I never went. I've been in California. Rosa's here with me. Can we come up there? We have to meet somebody in midtown in a couple of hours and I think you might want to come along anyways."

"Come on up, I'll order room service lunch."

"You hungry?" Lucy said to Rosa. She shook her head. "Order salads, Maggie. We'll be there in half an hour." Lucy freshened up and then gently helped sad, sorrowful Rosa out the door. Halfway down she banged on Jane's door. Jane answered. "Listen, honey, I'm back but I can't take— hey, pup, how are you," she interrupted herself as Claud jumped into the doorway. "Hey, baby."

"He's a great dog, but he's definitely yours, Lucy," said Jane. "He hasn't taken his eyes off the door. When I opened it to go out for a walk he went upstairs instead of down."

"I'll be back for him in a couple of hours, okay?"

"Sure. Back off, Claud," she said, nudging him back and edging the door shut. "Call me when you get home."

They taxied to the Waldorf and made their way to Maggie's room. Maggie let them in and hugged Lucy, then Rosa. Then, over salad served in silver bowls, they brought each other up to date. Maggie had been holed up in a tent on the edge of the Serengeti ever since she'd cut out of town the day they killed her brother. She had decided to stop collecting, and now planned to dedicate the rest of her life to saving wildlife all over the world. "When Nathaniel told me that he'd done what he'd done so that I could get those pieces, of course I denied it," she said. "But there was a grain of truth in it. That grain was the bullet that killed him, Lucy. And I might as well have pulled the trigger."

"Jesus, don't be so hard on yourself, Maggie," Lucy said. "You didn't ask him to drag those maniacs into your life."

"I know, but—hell, Rosa, I'm sorry about Darren," Maggie said. "I truly am. Just goes to show, like the lady said, 'A good man is hard to find.'"

"Apparently it's impossible, as a matter of fact," Rosa said. She was cheering up just a little. "So now what are we going to do, Lucy? I think I need a nap. This is all too much."

"Visit Mr. Insurance Man, and see what he has to tell us. By the way, he's about thirty and really cute," said Lucy.

"I'll save the nap for later," said Rosa. "Let's hit it."

They walked down to the Brueton Company and were shown in to Kelly Wyatt's office immediately. Lucy quickly introduced the two women, and explained who they were. Wyatt agreed that they could be in on his show and tell.

"Now then," he said. "Ever since you came by the other day, Lucy, I've been a little bugged about this Desert Gallery deal. Frankly, I threw that question at you about the artifacts because I wanted an answer as much as you probably do. So, I decided that maybe I shouldn't leave it up to you to find that answer, since it is after all my job, and so I started looking myself. There was no way I could ever involve the cops and get a warrant to search her house on Park Avenue, or their country house, or her husband's office downtown. By the way, he's a senior partner, with fiscal liability, in an investment firm that is up to its neck in bad debt thanks to some really stupid merger and acquisition activity. But my recent meetings with Madeleine Rooney did convince me that she is an arrogant bitch, arrogant to the point where she feels invulnerable, in some weird way. I mean part of it is just that Upper East Side mentality, but there's something more than that with her, something almost pathological. So like any good investigator unable to get in the front door I went around back, and started looking in the most obvious place—the trash. And you know what? There was nothing at the gallery, of course, she wouldn't have dreamed of dumping them there, but I paid a super a good tip and had a hell of a time rooting around in a Dumpster behind the building the Rooneys live in on Park Avenue. I got there too late to find the main haul, and I wasn't about to chase a bag of trash through the ten million cubic tons of garbage at Fresh Kills. But look what I found in the bottom of the Dumpster." He held up a fragment of dark red ceramic.

"Let me see that," said Margaret, reaching for it. She took it, examined it closely. "Looks like—"

"A piece of this!" Wyatt said triumphantly, throwing open a copy of the Desert Gallery catalogue and pointing at one of the photographs Lucy had taken in the gallery. "The Fertility Goddess Ixchell. Look at the way the fold in her garment goes right there," he said, pointing at the picture. "That's gotta be the same piece."

"Well, could be," Maggie said, "but—"

"No 'could-bes' about it. Our photo expert already verified that this is a fragment of that piece. And so we took it and had it dated by thermoluminescence," he said. "It is less than one year old. If things go the way I think they will, Madeleine Rooney's claim is dead in the water, and so's her credibility and her reputation. We're debating on whether or not to press charges or just let the whole thing sink out of sight. But either way, thanks to you I saved Brueton a million bucks, and I'm very popular around here as a result." He smiled. "Can I possibly buy you all a drink, if not dinner at Bouley?"

It was four p.m. The three women agreed to meet the insurance man at Bouley at eight-thirty for dinner on him. Why not? It was one of the best restaurants in town, none of them had ever been there, and he apparently knew somebody well enough to get a table on five hours' notice. No mean feat. They headed downtown by cab, got snagged in a gridlock, and arrived home at five. The trucks were roaring on Broome and Broadway, but for the moment, anyway, it was music to Lucy's ears as she led them up the stairs, stopping en route to pick up Claud the dog.

Lucy reached the door, started to unlock it, and realized she'd forgotten to lock it when she'd left. "Damn," she said, pushing the door open. "One of these days I'm gonna be real sorry about being so casual about this—" She stopped as she entered the room, followed by Maggie and Rosa. Darren Davidson sat on the couch facing the door. His arms were folded across his chest, and he looked grim.

"Hello, Lucy, Maggie. Rosa. Rosa, you're safe. Thank God." He leaped to his feet. "I don't know why you left, you don't have to explain anything, but I'm here to take you home."

"I can't go back with you, Darren," she said quietly, interrupting him. "I'm sorry, but—"

"What are you talking about?" he said. "What did you tell her, Lucy? What have you done to her?"

Rosa wouldn't look at him. "Play him the tape, Lucy. Just play him the stinking tape."

Lucy turned on the tape recorder. They listened together, the four of them silent. At the end, Darren got up. "So what's the big deal? I got involved in a little art scam."

Rosa spit out the words. "'A little art scam!' Those guys tried to kill me. They killed Maggie's brother, and those two men in Santa Fe. And you knew! Darren, you knew!"

"What the fuck was I supposed to do? You've got your million in the bank, and I've got a run-down house and twenty-five grand, Rosa. Easy for you to tell me what I should or shouldn't do. Easy for you to—Fuck this, you're coming with me," he snarled, and pulled out a pistol. He pointed it at Lucy. "You stupid bitch, if you hadn't come sniffing around none of this shit would have had to happen. Can't you see, Rosa, it's her fault." He moved over by Rosa, took her arm, and moved toward the door. "So let's just get the hell out of here and then we'll figure it out."

Leaping through the doorway to tackle Darren to the ground came Harold Ipswich, a huge bunch of forgive-me-Lucy flowers scattering across the room ahead of him. A shot went off, shattered a window. The women screamed. The gun followed the flowers through the air across the room as Harold tangled with Darren on the floor in a thrashing flurry. Darren was younger but Harold had the benefit of martial arts training he'd picked up along the undercover highway. He had Darren armlocked on his face, under control, in less than a minute.

"My God," said Rosa, staring down in shock at Darren, mashed on the floor. "To think I—hey, thanks, you pig," she said to Darren. "Thanks for pulling that ugly stunt, and making it that much easier for me to walk away from you." With that, she burst into tears. Lucy grabbed her in a hug. Silently Darren glared up at them, his head on the floor under Harold's knee.

Lucy didn't want to call the cops, but Rosa insisted, and after a while two uniforms and a detective came puffing up the stairs. After hearing the story they took Darren away. Rosa was sad but angry, and a resilient girl. She insisted on going to Bouley that night. Only change in plans was they had to make room at the table for Harold, who drank seltzer all night.

Lucy re-read the brief letter before sending it off.

Dear Heidi:

The article you assigned me has been transformed into a book, for which I have received a contract and an advance. As a result I will be unable to complete the assignment per our original agreement. Naturally I don't expect any kill fee whatsoever, and I will cover my incurred expenses. However, if you would like to discuss serialization rights, please feel free to call my agent, Dorothy LeMoyne, at the Figgs-Rider Agency. Meanwhile, I hope all is well. I'll send you an invite when the publication party date is set.

Regards,

Lucy Ripken

*A preview of the next
Lucy Ripken mystery*

The X Dames

by J. J. Henderson

1

Escape from New York

Lucy happened to be standing in the kitchen staring at the main event, a semi-defrosted package of sliced turkey breast, when Harry called at nearly five p.m.—unforgivably late as usual—to make excuses for not making it to dinner that night, voice space-crackling through a cell phone from somewhere in the vicinity of Caracas, Venezuela. Or so he claimed. Before she could hang up on him, he got his story going and she had to admit it was a good one. It seems, he told her, that these two dope guys he knew from his bad old days in Provincetown once upon a time had buried a million in cocaine-generated cash in heavy-duty plastic bags exactly one hundred twenty meters due north of the northeast corner of a gas station on the edge of a small town called Snake Creek, near the northern edge of Everglades National Park. So they'd told him, years back.

The first guy had his head blown off in a dope-related shoot out on a Bahama islet on New Year's Eve in 1999, and now Harry's sources had the second guy dead, heart stopped by a self-injected speedball sitting with the shades drawn, mid-day in a West Hollywood apartment. A miserable fate for a guy pushing sixty, Harry noted; but in any case, he went on, they'd told him about the stash of cash at least ten years ago, when he was in transition from bad boy to good cop, and at the time they'd both insisted, should they bite the dust, that no else knew and he should help himself to the money when the statute of limitations ran out. Now they were dead and it had. Harry didn't see a whole lot of excess moral weight attached to the bags of cash, and so—"Harry, that's enough," Lucy said. "Just cut me ten percent for stress and suffering when you dig it up."

"No problem, Luce," he said. "I could even go twelve. But there's more. Because once I was there, in Florida I mean, guess what? Or should I say guess who," he added, intriguingly, "Got me from Florida to Venezuela?" He paused. "Do the initials MV ring any chimes?"

"MV?" Lucy pondered. A truck squalled downstairs, gridlocked. "God, I've got to get out of here," she said. "I'm going utterly insane." A light dawned. "Maria Verde? You're after Maria Verde?"

"Was," Harry said, disappointment surfacing. "There was a reported sighting. I was in Florida to organize my dig—unfortunately the gas station is gone, in fact the tire department of a Wal-Mart appears to be positioned precisely atop the spot where the cash is supposedly buried, so I think it might stay buried for a while yet—when my *amigo Rogelio el Camaron*—"

"Roger the Shrimp?" Lucy said. "This is a guy you never mentioned before."

"He is possessed, they say, of the largest tool in Latin America."

"And proud of it no doubt."

"He used to be a cop. Now he's a porn star, hefting the heaviest wood south of the Rio Grande. But he's always done right by me, from way back when. And naturally I had red flagged that psycho-bitch, right after Jamaica. So Roger called to inform me that a person looking very much like our Maria recently had been seen on a plane headed out of Rio bound for Caracas. There was even video footage from an airport security camera. I saw it, and I do believe it was possibly her, although the shades and hair were very large. So I zipped down, only to find the trail gone cold. But here I am."

"Yes, there you are," said Lucy. "And here I am, not liking the thought of Maria Verde one bit, and wondering who's going to help me eat the three pounds of turkey fajitas I planned on cooking."

"Your friend Mickey seems to have a reliable appetite," Harry said.

"That's true—or was true, anyways, until she recently started taking antidepressants and went on a crash-and-burn diet."

"Mickey on a diet! You're kidding!"

"Her butt had gotten epic, Harry. And now the girl has lost twenty-seven pounds. Some kind of South Beach meets Atkins meets Weight Watchers in hell. She's on drugs, plus she met a guy and got inspired. No booze, no carbs, no fat, no fun, God, the forbidden list is endless. She's not good company right now, to tell the truth. I think when she hits 140 or so she'll start eating again. Or if he dumps her like the usual suspects usually do. Meanwhile—"

"Hey, sorry, Luce. Really. Trust me. I am not in Venezuela because I want to be."

"Sure, Harry. I'll share dinner with the dog." She sighed. "At least he's reliable."

"What can I say, it's—"

"I know, I know, not your fault. Listen, call me when you get back. I gotta go."

"Later Luce." He hung up. She clicked off and almost threw the phone. Damn that guy. Why did she still see him, when she never knew when she'd see him again?

The word for this moment was—whatever. She poked the turkey breast. It hadn't really defrosted. She shoved it back in the freezer, bagged all the neatly sliced and diced vegetables and put them in the refrigerator, stuck her cell phone in her purse, then took off her sexy black translucent lounging jammies and put on a pair of modified homeboy street pants, cut to ride high because Lucy was decidedly not into butt cleavage or pubic hairstyling. She added a neo-hippie beaded top, a little black sweater, her black cat's eye glasses, and open-toed sandals, for the late April breeze wafting in the windows carried early hints of summer. She woke the sleeping poodle with a "Yo, Claud, wanna hit it?" He leaped up and scrambled for the door. She checked makeup, brushed her currently medium-long blond hair back, did lipstick, grabbed leash and purse and headed out, not forgetting to lock the door.

She tripped five flights down—the elevator had been out of commission for a month—and out the building door onto her beloved, kinetic, once-funky Broadway, transformed, before her very eyes, from downscale shopping paradise to street-front shopping mall. Pseudo-hip corporate retail stores lined the street on both sides, in both directions, as far as her eye could see. Chasing after trendiness by moving into SoHo, these enterprises ended up chasing the trendies right out of the neighborhood. But that had been going on downtown long before Lucy Ripken had moved in, and she knew it was the inevitable evolution of the city. If bands of murderous, airplane-hijacking suicidal terrorists couldn't change the economic dynamic, no one could. And they had failed, thank God. But still, the damned street used to have some soul, or at least some cheap places to buy clothing and food, and now it was ruled by corporate retail.

She leashed the big white poodle, quite dashing with his newly shorn spring hair and his brilliant brown eyes, and walked west on Broome, then north on Wooster and west on Spring, dodging the packs of irksome wannabe hipsters and overdressed Eurotrash shoppers and noisy New Jersey noshers and the occasional haunted-looking longtime SoHo resident, belatedly maneuvering baby- and grocery-packed stroller home through the once serene, dignified blocks. Lucy was headed for the sylvan banks of the Hudson, and on the way she emptied herself of all the things that currently worried her: Harry, the demise of her neighborhood, the flatlining sales of her Mexican book, the state of the union and the world. A girl could go nuts pondering the last, she thought, then let it go as a warm breeze rippled over from the river. On the other hand, she couldn't quite let go of the image of Maria Verde, with her cockeyed Kewpie-doll grin, snarling in Jamaican moonlight as she pointed a gun at Lucy's heart. Lucy had been maybe ten seconds from dead when Harry's "associate" Prudence Fallowsmith, Jamaican cop, had tackled the raving, gun-toting bitch, saving Lucy's life. Maria Verde, whose drug deal Lucy and Harry had foiled, disappeared up the beach, and that was the last Lucy had seen or heard of her until today. They had stopped the drug deal, but still, Maria Verde had gotten away with murder.

In the soft spring evening, with traffic hushed to a white roar, and the crowds of SoHo now behind her, Lucy let Maria Verde go as well.

Soon she crossed the Westside Highway, and turned south on the ped and bike path. Forty minutes from her noisy front door, she settled on a bench under the lush green trees of Battery Park City. She gazed out, watching boats slide up and down the river as the lights of Jersey City rose before her.

As she considered what to do about dinner, and Claud lazily chased the odd squirrel, and children played amidst the quirky bestiary of miniature statues in the park, she loved New York again for a minute. Then her cell phone rang, an organ riff snatched from an ancient Los Lobos song, "Kiko and the Lavender Moon." She quickly fished it out of her purse and flipped it open. "Lucy here."

"That would be Lucy Ripken?"

"Yeah. Who's calling?" A female, didn't sound like a telemarketer but you never knew.

"Hey chill out. It's me. Terry. Teresa MacDonald, you paranoid dame."

"Terry! Hey!" Terry lived in L.A., wrote art criticism, had dated eccentric art-world celebs for years, and ranked among the smartest people Lucy knew. A still-skinny re-formed anorexic, red-haired, athletic, neurotic as hell but loads of fun. They'd met when Lucy did a piece for an L.A. magazine called *SCRUB*, devoted to bathing arcana, that had a moment of trendy glory and then went down the drain when the publisher made the mistake of moving the operation to New York, where the sharks made short work of it. Terry had been the culture editor in *SCRUB*'s glory years. Year. *SCRUB* was a short-lived phenom. Lucy had the complete set of back issues in a small box stuck in the depths of her closet. But she and Terry had stayed friendly. "What's up, girl?"

"Not too much. Still working on Milton Schamberg."

"God, how's that going?" A few years ago, Terry had started on an exhaustive biography of an obscure mid-twentieth-century Southern California painter whom she decided had played a far larger role in the cultural evolution of Los Angeles than anyone knew. It was taking forever.

"I'm into his thirties, so . . . "

"Since he died at forty-four you must be close."

"But the good parts are still to come."

"Right. The sixties and all that. Have you managed to get anyone to underwrite you yet?"

"Grants are fewer and farther between than ever, especially in publishing, so the short answer is no. But—and this is why I'm calling you, Lucy. I've been scrambling for money as usual, and thanks to Milton's son—"

"His son?"

"He's a Hollywood guy. In his forties—or fifties. Who can tell around here? Anyway he's a sick fuck but connected. So anyways I've got an interesting offer, and as soon as I heard it I thought of you."

"Really? What's the deal?"

"What do you think of when I say X Dames?"

"X Dames? Um—pompous porn stars?"

"No, you goon. Don't you know about the X Games?"

"Sure. That's like radical skateboarding, right?"

"And snowboarding, surfing, mountain biking, kite sailing—all those crazy sports that started in Southern California and are now taking over the world. At least those parts wired for cable."

"So—"

"Mix that with buff babes in bikinis and voilà: a new reality TV show coming soon to your local cable channel, to be called *The X Dames*. A bunch of cute athletic women—a shifting cast of characters, depending on the sport and the locations and the available breast-enhanced-yet-athletic broads, I suspect—travel around to different places and engage in competitions. Surfing, biking, whatever. Between contests they're theoretically up to the usual backbiting, catfighting, bitch-slapping, and the other thrills and chills that make reality TV so enticing. To win *dolares*, trips to exotic foreign lands, dates with C-list TV actors. It's basic trash, but there's cash behind this trash, it seems kinda fun, and I have been anointed an associate producer-slash-writer with hiring power. So—you want a job?"

"You want to hire me? To do what?" Lucy stood and walked over to the railing to look down into the dark waters of the river. This was getting interesting.

"Reality TV is not always reality, Luce. I'm sure you know that. And this particular show is going to be fairly heavily scripted. But for some obscure reason they want to use only writers who've never worked in The Industry—hence the hire of yours truly, since I have never been near the TV biz, as you know—and the green light for me to hire you."

"So where does Milton Junior fit in?"

"He's the man behind the brilliant idea. He lives on top of Tuna Canyon, in his dad's old house."

"Right, the one that looks like a flying saucer. Isn't that where—"

"His mother fell to her death."

"Or was pushed."

"That's in my next chapter. But junior—his name is Bobby Schamberg, by the way, not Milton—doesn't seem to have a problem living with mommy's ghost. Especially since the pad has five bedrooms and a pool and views of the ocean you wouldn't believe. The original American Schambergs made it big in lighting fixtures in Chicago a hundred years ago, and Milton surprised us all—well, me, anyway, since I always assume little-known artists must be

236 J. J. Henderson

236   J. J. Henderson

starving—by being, behind his Bohemian façade, a stock market whiz. He left a pile of dough that Bobby's been spending as fast as he can trying to play Hollywood. He's got a production company and thus far he's done a pair of seriously bad cable TV movies and a few sitcom pilots. *The X Dames* is his latest gambit. His ex-wife and current partner used to be a surfing champion, and they came up with the concept together. Since I was a writer and they knew me—I've been nosing around their lives for several years now, researching the book, and I think Bobby actually trusts me—they approached me, and I kind of helped them organize the initial proposal. Maybe they knew I needed money and did it out of pity. I don't know. In any case, they found some backers, pitched the thing to the Outside Network, where Bobby had a friend, and the next thing you know they got green-lighted and I got a sort of— job." She stopped. Lucy waited. "So what do you think?"

"Does this mean I get to get out of New York for the summer?"

"Like next week. Now. And you can bring your dog. I've got you set up in a studio two blocks from the beach in Venice if you take the offer. It's tiny and two thousand a month but the producers are willing to pay you about five times that, at least while they get the thing off the ground. You've got a bit of a rep thanks to the Mexico book— speaking of which, we have to go to Mexico right away because they want to jump-start the show by staging a surfing contest in this little town north of Puerto Vallarta called Sayulita, and they tell me it's a north and west swell beach, so the waves will stop breaking once summer settles in."

"Jesus," said Lucy, awash in immediate and very cool possibilities. L.A., working in TV, good money, another trip to Mexico, but this time the west coast, keeping those Isla Mujeres ghosts at bay a thousand miles away. A job! "It sounds too good to be true. Wow, Terry, I can't believe you pulled this off."

"I can't either. It fell on my head like a gold brick."

"I should say let me think about it for a couple of days but I'm more inclined, right now, to say, see you next week. I just have to deal with my loft and—"

"Perfect. I'll tell them to email you a draft contract. You can read it, make changes, print it out, sign it, and send it back to me. Trust me, it'll treat you right."

"*Bueno*. And Terry, thanks for thinking of me."

"I've seen you on a sailboard, Luce. You could probably be an X Dame yourself, were you so inclined."

"No way, Ter. I'm pushing thirty-five and way too Manhattanized for competition sports."

"But still, you know your way around the ocean."

"I guess. Listen, I gotta go get a bite. My dinner guest—none other than the fabulous Harry Ipswich—putzed out on me, so I'm wandering the streets in search of food."

"Again!? Doesn't he do that all the time?"

"His schedule is—unpredictable. And so I suffer. Instead of cooking for him I'm going to my favorite bistro and see what looks good. Wish you could join me."

"Cook up an X Dame location in New York and I will. Meanwhile next week we'll make the L.A. dining rounds. I still hate TV, but it is nice to be getting a lot of money for a little work."

"Instead of a little money for a lot of work, the writer's usual fate. See you then." Lucy shut her phone, jumped up and clicked her heels together, then laughed out loud. "Claud, we are moving to Southern California!"

Fifteen minutes later, as she tethered Claud to a street-lamp and strolled into The Frog's Grotto, her Tribeca bistro of the moment, it dawned on her that at ten grand a month she'd make her twelve percent of Harry's buried million in a year. She had no illusions that the gig would last that long, but even a couple of months at ten thousand per would add up to a pile of money. And getting out of Manhattan for the summer was, quite simply, priceless.

When Harry showed up three days later, tanned, tired, dirty, and bug-bitten, Lucy couldn't help but feel a low glimmer of satisfaction when she told him she was moving to L.A. for a while. "And of course you're welcome to the loft, as always," she added, handing him an ice-crusted shot glass of his favorite vodka. Harry had a mouse-sized fourth floor East Village walk-up, a *tres chic* locale but lacking air conditioning, with a tub in the kitchen and toilet down the hall, so staying at Lucy's loft, with or without her there, was like vacation for him. "And you don't even have to deal with the dogster. He's going with me, eh what, Claud? He'll be thrilled to see you when you come visit."

"Not so fast, kiddo," Harry said, and knocked back the shot. "Whooo, that's good." She poured him another. "Aside from the fact that I think you're crazy to go out there—L.A. is an inferno, Luce, and the TV industry inhabits the ninth circle—I've got my own out-of-town gig going. As it turns out, I'm on assignment in Florida for a while."

"What? What kind of assignment? You said you were done with Florida for now."

"Well, actually I volunteered for surveillance duty on a couple of illicit landing strips in the jungle not far from Snake Creek. My cover is I'm doing a piece on Everglades National Park for an airline magazine. But there is a ton of dope coming into the area by plane all the time, so I'll have my hands full. Who knows, I might even stop a few hundred pounds of coke or junk from finding its nasty way up here. But aside from that and the writing gig, the real reason I set it up is I've come up with a plan. I've been contemplating that Wal-Mart situation I told you about, with the million bucks, and I think I know a way to get at the money without—"

"You can't be serious, Harry. I've never been in a Wal-Mart but I imagine there's probably fifty tons of concrete sitting on top of your mythical bags of money, plus security up the wazoo."

"Exactly. Security. As in seriously underpaid dudes in blue shirts with tin badges who would probably be very happy to get ten percent of my gross in exchange for getting me floor and fixture plans, and maybe running some cover, so that when I dig my tunnel from the swamp behind the back of the building I won't hit any cables, pipes, or people. I checked it out. There's a thick stand of jungle back there and the tunnel will only have to be about sixty or seventy feet long."

"A seventy-foot tunnel under a Wal-Mart superstore? Harry, you're nuts. This sounds like a really dumb-ass plan."

"You know what, Luce? Believe it or not I'm sick of being broke all the time. Sick of living in that overpriced rat hole on East Seventh. I need a leg up and those guys weren't bullshitting me. The money's there for the taking, it's not stealing, and I'm the only person on the planet who knows about it. Excepting you, of course."

"It's a hare-brained scheme, Harry, and you know it. Besides, what am I going to do about the loft? Who can I get to stay here? I depend on you for this. You know I can't just advertise for a subletter. Not with the landlord situation."

"Hey, you're going to be working in TV. Making major money, right? If I were you, I'd just leave it empty. You can afford six hundred a month for the peace of mind."

She hadn't thought of that. Maybe it was true. She just wasn't used to that kind of spare cash. "Well, I'm going to make a few calls, see if I can round up someone trustworthy. If not, I guess I could just lock the door and walk away."

"Ask Jane downstairs to keep an eye on the place. She's kind of a friend, right? But I would take all your valuables and personal stuff. You never know what that fucking landlord might try."

Soon they cut the chatter and commenced with peeling each other's clothing off, a ritual that had only improved with time. By now, two years into it, they knew each other's hot spots, when and how to hit them. They spent that night together, and had great sex. Twice, with a vodka break between. Not at all bad for a fortysomething man and a thirtysomething girl. Even if she did kinda watch the clock, wondering. If her time was running out. Time for what? Love and marriage and a baby carriage? Who knew any more these days?

Whatever Harry had in the way of failings, he was a wonderful lover and had been since their very first nights together in Jamaica. Lucy suspected his unpredictable avail-ability had something to do with it—that hoary old cliché, absence makes the heart grow fonder, having some bearing on the situation. He was definitely absent.

Come morning, Harry went off to his East Village dump to prep for his own incipient departure back to the Florida swamps, and Lucy got on the phone to chase after subletters while breaking out her three suitcases and two duffel bags, having decided to do a major reassessment of her worldly goods, so that what she took to California would be all that she held dear, and what she left behind would be the basics.

Everything else she bagged for throwaway, including the collected back issues of *SCRUB* magazine. By the time she was ready to go a week later, she had sixteen bags of trash, five overstuffed suitcases, and a loft that had never looked better—empty of everything but furniture, a couple of prints, her five-year-old dinosaur desktop PC—drained of all her files—and the essentials in the kitchen and bathroom.

She never did find anyone she trusted enough to sublet or loft-sit. In the first week of May—with a signed hard copy of her $2,500-per-week X Dames contract in her carry-on and a backup in her laptop—on the day before her depar-ture to L.A., she ambled downstairs and after walking Claud around the block, she went into the building next door. She tied Claud up and ascended to the second floor, where the bad-cop landlord, Itzak Lascovich, ran his business, SeaBee Fabric Merchants, out of a grubby little office in the corner of a dingy, fluorescent-lit, six-thousand-square-foot loft crammed with chaotically heaped twelve-foot rolls of cheap fabric. He dealt primarily with wholesalers in Africa, he claimed, but it was strange—in all her years in the loft she had never actually seen any fabric go into, or out of, his place of business. Only him, scurrying about in his rodent-like fashion.

She picked her way through the stacks of rolled fabric until she could see him through the dirty glass door of his office. He was greenish under the twittering lights, barking at someone on the phone, pushing his greasy white hair back with a clawlike hand. She tapped on the glass. He looked up, waved her in, continued barking. She opened the door. His wife—twice his size, thin brown hair pulled back tight, gaudy lipstick in place, tree-trunk legs nicely stockinged and crossed—never said a word and sat there vigilant as she did all day every day. She glared at Lucy briefly, then returned her gaze to the middle distance. Lascovich waved at the one chair not covered by papers, fabric samples, his skinny ass, or his wife's fat one. Lucy sat, feeling rather sassy in spite of the grim vibe in the grim little room. How they could spend fifty or sixty hours a week in this hole she had never figured out. "Goodbye," he said to the phone, then hung up. "So Miss Lucy Ripken it is the third of May you haf my rent?"

"I do, yes." She put the check on his desk. He picked it up, looked at it, frowned, and shook his head. "Sometime you will pay market value, Miss Lucy Ripken."

"Not this year." She smiled at him. "Don't forget it was you that initiated the lawsuit, Izzy."

"You are illegal. The whole lot of you. And I will get my buildink back sometime."

"Well, maybe so, but not today. Oh, by the way," she went on, hoping her casual tone would carry the moment. She had decided that though it would be risky to reveal her plans, it would be better than having Jane spring it on him after she was gone. This way, at least, she would have some idea of his response—and she could then deal accordingly. "I wanted to let you know that I'm going to be traveling for a while, and the place won't be occupied. But I will be paying rent, through Jane Aronstein, so you don't need to—"

"You can't go away and keep my floor for you to come back and—"

"Of course I can, Itzak. I will be paying the rent and—"

"If the place is not occupied then I am having it."

"I don't think so, Mr.—"

"I don't care what you are thinking, I am—"

"This conversation is over, Iz. I'll have my lawyer call you."

"No. I will be taking the place when you—"

"Good day, Mrs. Lascovich," she said, and breezed out. Then stormed down the stairs. "Damn," she said to Claud as she unhooked his leash from the banister, slammed out the door, and stood on the Broadway sidewalk, trying to collect herself. "Goddamn, pup," she said. "That guy is so infuriating."

She went into her own building, hiked up to her loft, and got on the phone with Jack Harshman, who'd been her legal pit bull on matters residential since the day she moved into the loft and Lascovich tried to evict her.

Later, after hours, she put all of her trash out on the street in black plastic bags, and then she did what Harshman had advised. She spent two hundred and fifty dollars to have a locksmith come over and hike up the stairs and change one of the three locks on her door and on the door inside the elevator at the other end of the loft. She gave a set of new keys to her downstairs neighbor Jane, with strict instructions not to let Lascovich or anyone else have them under any circumstances. Jane had been in the building even longer than Lucy so she got it. Lucy pocketed the other set.

After a less-than-rousing overnighter with Harry, whose excessive, mournful vodka drinking rendered him entirely incapable, they left for La Guardia at seven a.m., she with five suitcases and a carry-on containing her camera and laptop. Harry had a single carry-on. His Miami flight left at nine-thirty, half an hour before Lucy's L.A. flight. They got their cell numbers and tentative plans to meet organized and said goodbye, Harry's hangdog, hungover face the unfortunate last image Lucy and the drugged and caged Claud had of him as he forlornly headed off to find his boarding gate. As he disappeared into the crowd charging through the terminal, Lucy found it hard to believe he was actually going to Florida to burrow a tunnel under the back end of a Wal-Mart in search of a plastic bag with a million dollars inside. She, on the other hand, had a contract and a check for eleven thousand dollars in her pocket, a one-month advance from the producers of *The X Dames*. They had thrown in the extra thousand in moving expenses, and so after checking her bags, and dishing out a fifty-dollar tip to make sure Claud got treated right en route, and doing security, and hitting the latte stand, and grabbing a *Times* from the concourse newsstand, and waiting for half an hour at the gate, Lucy pre-boarded with the gilded gang, and traveled first class for the first time in her life. She was going Hollywood.